Christmas Key

A Tropical Noel Adventure

Kirk Jockell and Mac Fortner

THE FREE MULLET PRESS, LLC

Copyright © 2023 by Kirk S. Jockell and Mac Fortner

All rights reserved.

ISBN: 978-1-963656-25-1 (paperback version)

Book Design by The Free Mullet Press, LLC

Cover Design by Barefoot Book Productions

Kirk Photo by Debbie Hooper Photography

Mac Photo by Cindy Fortner

*Christmas Key i*s a work of fiction. Names, characters, places, and incidents, except where indicated, are either products of the author's imagination or used fictitiously. Any resemblance to actual events or locales or persons (except for Santa Claus), living or dead, is strictly coincidental. No portion of this book may be reproduced in any form without written permission from the publisher or author, except as permitted by U.S. copyright law.

PRINTED IN THE UNITED STATES OF AMERICA

The small town square was lit with twinkling Christmas lights as people walked home from work, and the smell of roasting chestnuts drifted through the air. A man paused outside the soup kitchen to hand out scarves to those who waited in line. Across town, a group of volunteers sang carols at a nursing home, and a family drove around delivering groceries to those in need. Everywhere you looked, there were acts of kindness being done in the spirit of the season.

This book is dedicated to all of you who generously give year round - your compassionate actions bring light into darkness and hope into despair.

One

Part I: Nigel Logan

I leaned over and turned my head to watch. Two rival biker guys faced off. Their right hands clasped together, elbows planted firmly on the bar where the wager, a pile of cash, lay. Even I put in a fifty-spot to sweeten the kitty. Now and then, someone else would slip a bill or two in there. It was quite the show.

Each fella met the other with locked eyes and clenched teeth as they growled and grunted at one another. Large beads of sweat built and rolled down their foreheads. Yelling and cheers filled the room from the spectators, some wearing festive colors, some clad in Santa suits and others dressed as elves. The band stopped playing their Christmas songs. It was useless. They could barely hear themselves. Both men had a comrade or two, screaming demands and encouragement into their ears.

One yelled, "COME ON, DAMMIT! PUSH, BUBBA! PUSH!"

The other bellowed, "STAY ON HIM, TANK! DON'T GIVE AN INCH! GO! GO! GO!"

The tattoos on their forearms and biceps twitched and moved around their bulging veins. It couldn't stay in a stalemate forever. Eventually, something had to give, and it did. Bubba screamed in agony as Tank's arm moved. The entire room chanted. "Bubba! Bubba! Bubba!"

I smiled as the back of Tank's wrist inched closer and closer to the bar. Then it stopped, just short of a Bubba victory.

Bubba yelled even louder in a final attempt to put his rival down. But obviously, Tank wasn't done. He was extremely quiet and focused as Bubba screamed for strength. Then... Tank closed his eyes. Moments later, the gains enjoyed by Bubba retreated, and the chanting switched to Tank. "Tank! Tank! Tank!" People threw more money on the pile.

I mumbled, "Dang."

Their hands returned to the neutral position, but only briefly. In a quick and decisive manner, the back of Tank's hand smacked the bar. The Christmas arm wrestling championship was over. Bubba rose, held his hands high in the air, and yelled, "Merry Christmas to all!" while the room chanted his name.

When I moved my eyes to check on the biker called Tank, I watched him rush from around the bar and push through the crowd toward Bubba, carrying a mistletoe above his head. *Oh, shit.* I wanted to intervene, but there was no way I could get through the crowd fast enough. It was that packed.

I watched Tank come up behind Bubba, grab him by the shoulder and swing him around, yelling, "You son of a Grinch!"

They stared and scowled at each other for a few beats. Then they broke out in laughter, collided into a bear hug, and patted each other on the back. I rolled my eyes.

As everyone celebrated, the bartender, Travis, grabbed the cash off the bar and counted it as he walked toward me. He stopped a few feet away, and I asked, "So? How much?"

He stopped counting and held up a finger. *Hold on!* When he finished, he looked at me and said, "Damn, looks like Santa's been very generous this year." Then he grabbed a whistle and blew short blasts to get the crowd's attention. The room went quiet. Travis held the fistful of bills high in the air and announced, "It's a record!" The room erupted again, and Travis used his hands to wave the crowd back down to silence. Then he raised his voice. "Seven hundred eighty-two dollars!"

Once again, the room went crazy with jubilation and excitement. If I'd ever seen a happier group of people, I couldn't remember when.

Travis put the wad of cash in his pocket and approached me.

"Nice way to kick things off, huh?" I asked.

"I'd say so. The organizers will be pleased." He looked at his watch, then over my shoulder, and continued. "They should be here soon."

I laughed. "You already have to be over capacity. If you pack any more people in here, the Fire Marshall is going to shut you down."

Travis laughed and pointed at a guy across the room. He appeared passed out. Standing, leaning back, holding up the wall. His chin was buried in his chest. "That's him over there. I think we'll be okay."

"Only in Key West," I said.

I couldn't remember the date. Come to think of it, I haven't known what day it was since late November when they flipped the big electrical breaker to power up the *Harbor Walk of Lights.* The electrification kicks off the holiday season and the Key West *Bight before Christmas* celebration. The island was in full swing with festive holiday spirit—as well as other spirits—with scheduled events to fill your calendar, occupy all your time, and drain your wallet through bringing in the New Year.

One of the many events was POSH (Paws Often Steal Hearts). It is an annual gala fundraiser to benefit the Florida Keys SPCA. They hold the formal event at the Audubon House on Whitehead Street, but the after-party continues a few blocks away at the infamous Green Parrot. That's where I sat, on my stool. Number seventeen.

"Would you like me to top off your drink?" asked Travis.

"I don't know if I can handle another Diet Coke, but yeah. Might as well live dangerously."

"That's just like you, Nigel. Always living on the edge."

I returned a sheepish smile. *If you only knew.*

After Travis squeezed a lime into my drink and put the soda gun back in its holster, a young man approached. He was handsome and in his late twenties, if I had to guess. Well-tanned and muscle-bound, sporting an orange tank top. I'd never seen him before, but Travis knew him.

"Hey, Tommy. Ready to do your thing?"

"That's why I'm here."

"His thing?" I asked.

"Yeah." Using his thumb to point, Travis said, "Once the big shots get here from the gala, Tommy does push-ups for money to help raise money for POSH. One dollar per push-up." He turned to look at Tommy. "How many did you do last year, a hundred and forty?"

"One forty-three," said Tommy, sounding a little put off that Travis forget those last three critical efforts.

"That's pretty impressive," I said. "What do you say we make it a competition? See who can do the most. Folks can wager on their favorite. Kind of like the arm-wrestling gig."

A sexy, sophisticated voice chimed in from behind me. "I would pay handsomely to see that."

I turned around and found a creature fitting for the voice. A tall, slim brunette with straight hair that framed her face and ended in a crop just above the shoulders. She wore a short, but eloquent, black sleeveless dress that ended above her knees and shapely calves. It hugged her features and complemented her small but perky breasts. Her stiletto heels added to her height and sex appeal. Adorning her head, a bright blue-feathered fascinator matched the color of her eyes in perfect coordination. She was stunning. I was speechless.

"Hello, Ms. Sylvia," said Travis. "So that would be something you'd like to see?"

"I believe so, Trav. I think the other gals would enjoy it too. That is..." She moved like a stalking cat as she drew nearer and felt my shoulders and ran her hand down my arm. Then her eyes met mine. "...if our stranger here can promise a good show."

Through my smile, I said, "I can hold my own."

She turned toward the orange tank top and said, "No offense, Tommy. The ladies and I have had fun watching you do your push-ups, but it gets boring after a while. Now, if we turn it into a horse race between two handsome hunks, wouldn't that be something?"

"No offense taken," said Tommy. "I'm game if he is."

She turned back toward me and said, "Well, I'm guessing he is. After all, it was his idea."

I said nothing but offered a wink.

"Good! Good! What's your name, sweetheart?"

Sweetheart. I found that an odd thing to call me. Especially since I probably had ten or more years on her. "The name is Logan. Nigel Logan."

"Just curious," she said. "How old are you?"

"I'm fifty. I turn fifty-one in March. Is that a problem?"

"Oh, no. That's perfect. Youth versus..."

"Experience," I interjected.

She returned a million-dollar grin and nodded as her tongue brushed across her upper lip. Then she turned to our barkeep. "Thanks, Trav. This is going to be fun. I'll talk it up with the rest of the ladies once they get here." She walked away. After a few steps, she stopped, turned around, winked at me and added, "But which horse to bet on? Now that is the question."

Two

Sylvia Mason was the first to arrive at the Green Parrot for the POSH after-party. More were on their way.

Travis explained that Sylvia was an accomplished, if not the most accomplished, real estate agent and developer in Key West. She was single. Formerly known as Sylvia Prescott. She took back her maiden name of Mason after divorcing her former husband and business partner. Once she learned he cooked the books, especially for his own benefit, she called in a savvy team of accountants from Atlanta. The guidance she gave them was clear: pore over every transaction, find where *my* money ended up, and provide *me* with enough evidence to kick the selfish, thieving bastard into poverty. When one accountant asked if she would really do that to her husband, she replied, "Am I paying you to ask stupid questions, or perhaps I've made a mistake and need to hire another firm?"

In the end, the team from Atlanta found that her husband, David Prescott, had tucked away and hidden from taxes over three million dollars. The three offshore shell companies that he controlled regularly sent bogus invoices to their firm, Prescott Enterprises, to which Mr. Prescott directed payment. He used the money sent to the shells to pay personal expenses, buy his Porsche 911, buy exclusive club memberships, and pay rent on a condo in South Beach where he frequently visited to entertain a laundry list of Miami women of the night. Not only did the scheme fund Mr. Prescott's shell companies, it also provided Prescott Enterprises with unfounded, illegal expenses.

Sylvia Prescott and her team of hotshot bean counters went directly to the IRS. As an innocent party to the dealings, she managed an amnesty deal in exchange for all her investigatory findings. Her only demand: prosecute the bastard to the fullest extent of the law. David Prescott still has three and a half years to serve of his five-year sentence.

As it would turn out, the stunning Sylvia was only an example of what would follow. Slowly, others from the big event filed in decked out in their formal and semi-formal attire. The men looked dapper, and the women were incredible. The place smelled of money, not that there wasn't already plenty there. Once inside, the wives dumped their husbands. The men meandered off to drink their whiskey, smoke their cigars, and tell magnificent lies.

I watched the ladies as they gravitated toward the former Mrs. Prescott. Sylvia collected all the beauties. I counted eight altogether. She was explaining the changes to the push-up program. The more she explained, the more her lady friends shot mischievous glances toward me and young Tommy.

I turned to Tommy. "I think we get to be the *meat market* tonight."

"That appears the case," said Tommy. "I don't mind. Maybe I'll get laid this year."

I chuckled, and Tommy said, "Here they come."

I turned to see Miss Sylvia lead her little tribe toward Tommy and me. She pushed other patrons around and out of the way to make room for her friends.

"Ladies... you all know our Tommy. He returned this year to do his push-ups and help raise money for our cause. But, let me introduce you to Mr. Logan. He..."

I stopped her. "Please... no mister stuff. Just call me Nigel. Or better still, Chief."

One lady said, "Oh, Nigel. I like that name."

Another, from the back of the pack, said, "No. He's Chief to me."

"Okay, you little vixens. Settle down," said Sylvia.

Giggles and snickers came from her group.

"As I was saying," she stopped to look at me before continuing. "Our Chief has challenged Tommy to a push-up competition. They will fight to see who can do the most. It will be our job to provide loads of financial support and encouragement. How does that sound?"

All the ladies agreed, and one said, "Why don't you tell us a bit about yourself, Nigel? We know nothing about you."

"There isn't much to tell. I'm a retired chief petty officer from the U.S. Navy, and I live on my sailboat. I like women, the smell of puppy breath, kittens, and..." I held up my glass. "Diet Coke."

A sexy blond from the back stepped up. "You said you like women. What about those of us that are more comfortable dressing the part?"

"Well," I said, "I'm big on honesty, so I'll just tell you. There isn't much my equipment can do to handle a situation like that. But..." I added a wink. "I got to tell you. If that's your case, you have your equipment working. That's for damn sure. Your hair and that red gown have you looking like a smoking-hot honey. And something else... if you're wearing any makeup, it doesn't show. Amazing."

The blond stepped closer and took my hands. "Oh, ladies! I have to say, the Chief is mighty dreamy."

Another voice called out. "That's just fine, Chuck. Now step back so we can get a better look."

Sylvia asked, "So, why are you wanting to do this, Chief?"

"Well, Tommy here is just hoping to get laid."

Tommy reached over and punched my arm. "Man! What the hell are you doing?"

I laughed. "Just kidding. Just kidding. Sorry, Tommy." I stopped laughing. "In all seriousness, I love the cause. Helping animals find loving homes in a world so willing to discard them and pretend they don't exist is a noble endeavor. You guys are heroes."

The ladies said nothing but nodded.

"So, ladies, my question to you is quite simple. Are you ready to turn loose of those burdensome dollars, all that moldy money that's just hanging around without a purpose?"

A gorgeous redhead with green eyes stepped up and asked, "So, why should we throw our support toward you?"

"In all honesty, I don't care if you cheer for me or Tommy. As long as the cash and the checks roll in, I'll be happy. But... if you need a reason to bet on me, I'll give you one."

I reached into my front pocket and pulled out a wad of folded cash. I dealt two hundred-dollar bills off the top and threw them on the bar. "Bet on me, because I'm willing to bet on myself."

The eyes of Sylvia's tribe opened wide. Then they looked at Tommy.

"What? Why are you looking at me?" asked Tommy.

I pulled off another hundred and said, "And... I'm betting on Tommy, too. How's that for a start? Now, when do we get this party started?"

Travis said that he wanted to kick things off at ten and that it would be a two-tier event. The first part would be to see which of us could get to a hundred push-ups first. Beyond that, it would be strictly based on volume.

"That's a pretty good idea, Travis," I said. "It adds a little endurance strategy."

"I can't take the credit. It was Sylvia's idea."

I looked at my watch. It was 2150. Ten minutes to show time. I asked for a tall glass of water, no ice, and downed it when it arrived. Tommy and I jumped up and sat on the bar so the ladies could have a last look at the goods. Even the guys took an interest in what was about to go down.

We each had a person dedicated to doing the counting so we could concentrate on the push-ups. As the top of the hour approached, Travis cleared the bar away to make room for us. I smiled at Tommy and extended a hand. "You ready?"

"Sure thing, old man. Good luck."

"I don't believe in luck."

"Okay, gentlemen," said Travis, "up on the bar."

The bar at the Green Parrot occupies the middle of the room and is basically a rectangular box. Tommy and I took up one of its corners, facing the vertex so we could eyeball each other.

"Up to the ready position!" yelled Travis.

Tommy and I popped up, faces forward.

"There is only one rule," said Travis. "They have to be good push-ups. Your elbows must meet or break forty-five degrees. Ready?"

Tommy and I nodded.

"Here we go. Fifteen, Fourteen, Thirteen"

While Travis whittled the clock down, Sylvia walked up to me, flashed a hundred-dollar bill under my chin, set it on the bar, and leaned in for a kiss. When we unlocked our lips, she said, "That's just for starters."

Oh, dear.

"Three, Two, One, Go!"

I let Tommy set the pace and matched him, push-up for push-up. I liked it. A reasonable rhythm. Somewhere around the count of twenty-five, Chuck, the sexy drag queen, dropped a fifty under my nose. I smiled and answered my appreciation by launching my hands off the bar and throwing in a clap before landing back into position. That got Tommy's attention. When he sent me a glance, I shot back with a wink.

It wasn't something I had planned to do, but the crowd seemed to enjoy it. Every time they threw money in the pot, I threw in a clapping push-up. The money started rolling in. At some point, after passing the sixty count, a guy walked up and said, "How long do you think you can keep that up?"

I said nothing but watched him pull a wad of bills out of his pocket. He fanned them out in front of me. Twenties. Then, for the next ten push-ups, he threw them down one by one. While I felt the burn, I gave him what he paid for and never lost pace with Tommy.

From behind the bar, Travis yelled, "Seventy-five!" The crowd loved it and cheers erupted.

The joyous, spirited environment came to a halt as a woman let out an earth startling scream. Another then joined her, then another. The room became chilly, and a foul feeling took hold. I tried to ignore it and focused on Tommy's pace, however; the crowd parted and gave me a clear view out the door and street. What I saw out on the sidewalk made me stop in the up position.

You never know what you are going to see on the streets of Key West. So much so that nothing should surprise you. From terrible-looking cross-dressers and public nudity disguised behind elaborate body paint, to dudes wearing nothing but flip-flops and G-strings, anything goes. After you've been here awhile, few things will make you do a double take. This time was different. The overwhelming realism was more than I could stand. I couldn't tell where the costume started or ended. A tall figure stood gazing into the bar. It had the head of a menacing, horrific goat, horns curled out from the top of its head. It stood erect, like a man on hooved feet. A large basket was strapped to its back. The long and pointed fingers of its hands clenched bundles of branches. It stepped just inside the door and swatted the branches at those around him. The joyous, celebratory mood was gone and replaced with the smell of hate and anger. Then he, she, *it* was gone.

What the hell?

The next thing I knew, I heard the voice of Sylvia screaming angrily in my ear. "What are you doing?"

I looked at her, then toward a smiling Tommy.

Crap! He's picked up his pace.

I heard the bean counter keeping track of my progress repeat himself. "Seventy-seven, Seventy-seven, Seventy-seven." Then I heard Tommy's guy report. "Eighty-one. Eighty-two."

Sylvia yelled, "Go, Nigel! Go!"

I did. Using my newfound anger, I hammered out my push-ups as fast as I could. Little by little, my deficiency decreased. *Damn*, I thought. *This Tommy is strong.*

"Eighty-nine!"

"Eighty-seven!"

Then I caught a break. I heard Tommy's count report twice, "Ninety-one. Ninety-one. Can't count that last one, Tommy."

"Ninety-two!"

"Ninety-one!"

Sylvia leaned in sounding more calm and confident. "Come on, baby. You can do it! I know you can."

She threw another hundred-dollar bill on the sweat-soaked pile of cash under my dripping nose, and I yelled, launching up to throw in a clap.

"That's my boy," she said.

Then I heard the counters say in unison, "Ninety-five."

It was a sprint to the finish. And I took off. At ninety-eight, I grabbed a slight lead by half a push-up. When my counter yelled, "One hundred!" I stopped to watch Tommy finish his last one. He stopped too.

My arms burned. I know Tommy's did too. We looked at each other, panting. He spat out, "Good job. Congratulations."

"Same to you. You're strong, boy. Damn strong."

"What happened earlier?" asked Tommy. "The room got weird. Cold and ugly."

I looked back out toward the door. "I'm not sure, but I felt it too."

Sylvia rubbed on my sweaty back and kissed me again.

When she came up for air, I said, "You're going to have to stop that if I am going to concentrate."

She winked and said, "Maybe in the morning."

Oh... My God.

"Don't get too comfortable, boys," said Travis, "you're not done. Round two is coming up soon."

While still in the up position, Tommy and I rocked back and forth so we could lift our arms to shake out some lactic acid and shake in some freshly oxygenated blood.

Round two was about stamina and endurance. I did not know how many push-ups I had left in my fifty-year-old body, but I was about to find out.

Three

Key West isn't my home, but you wouldn't know that based on how I've acted since arriving here back in the spring. No, home for me is still a stretch of the Florida Panhandle, the Forgotten Coast, specifically Port St. Joe. One day I'll go back, and I take comfort in thinking of that day, but it will have to wait. There are issues I still need to work through.

I arrived here on *MisChief*, my thirty-two-foot classic sailboat, along with a female companion, Emma. We shoved off from Port St. Joe as friends. Before making our arrival in the Keys, we ended up *really* close friends. Friends with benefits and no complications.

I came into her life when she needed someone. She came into mine when I needed a distraction.

When she met me, she had found herself in a physically abusive relationship with a younger man. He ended up being a double bastard. Not only had he hit her, but he was preparing to run off with over six figures of her money. A con, never to be seen again. I helped her make things right. It seems to be what I do, often at the cost of troubling, violent, and often deadly circumstances.

When I met Emma, one word described me: tormented. I struggled with facing my dark past and who I had become. Vigilante, rogue deliverer of justice, punisher of evil, whatever; I never wanted to be any of those things. Yet, here I am. A guy that does what needs doing, when I feel my back against a wall. Through it all, I lost my best girl, Candice, the love of my life. She saw me for what I had become and severed any thought of having a life together. Damn, that was over a year ago, and I still hurt, but I'm getting better. Thanks to Emma.

Emma was sixty-three, and I was fifty. Our ages weren't important to us, though she would jokingly call me her *boy toy*. If I played along and called her *my old lady*, she would often comment and say, "That's okay with me. I'm getting the better end of the deal." I wasn't so sure she was right about that.

She stayed with me for three weeks. On our last night together, we simply held each other through the night. I think we both felt that having sex one last time would cheapen our time together. It simply wasn't necessary for either of us. The next morning, we thanked each other for everything, said our goodbyes, and I watched as the wheels of her flight tucked themselves up into the fuselage.

When my eyes opened at four in the morning, I kept still, looked at the ceiling, and let my eyes adjust to the darkness. Then I gently raised up and rested on my elbows. With the help of a nearby nightlight, I took in the unfamiliarity of my surroundings until my memory backfilled. I lowered myself back onto the bed and turned on my side. The body next to me looked peaceful and at ease. Her breathing was slow and gentle. There was just enough light that I could make out her rapid eye movement. She was dreaming. As her eyes darted about, her mouth would tighten and twitch into small smiles. A thought crossed my mind. *Are you dreaming about me?*

She looked sweet and had acted that way since we left the crowds and the hustle and bustle of the after-party at the Green Parrot. Once behind closed doors, she never once put on her strong, businesswoman power act like she did earlier in the evening. I realized the public persona of Sylvia Mason was nothing like the genuine article. I can say I feel honored to have experienced both sides. I wanted to kiss her on the forehead, but I didn't. Afraid that I would wake her. *Let her rest.*

I moved like a cat as I crawled out of bed. The floor felt cool on my bare feet. I made my way to the door until I heard a groggy and broken voice behind me.

"Where are you going?"

I turned. "I'm sorry. I didn't mean to wake you."

"Are you leaving?"

I walked back over, sat on the bed, and with my fingers moved the strands of hair away from her face. "No. I'm not leaving. I would never leave without saying goodbye. That would be rude. I was just going to look for the coffeepot."

I had left folks without saying goodbye before, but under more dire circumstances. But, after the way things went last night, leaving without a proper goodbye was unthinkable.

She smiled. "What time is it?"

"It's a little after four. Close your eyes and get some sleep. I'll be here with hot coffee when you wake up."

"Four? Well, I typically get up at five, so I might as well get up too."

I helped her sit up, and watched as she rubbed her eyes.

"I bet I look like dog crap," she said with a chuckle.

"On the contrary."

She reached out and rubbed my arm. "You're so sweet." Then she fell backwards on the bed. "And absolutely amazing, too."

I felt myself blushing a bit. I'm not comfortable with women commenting on my performance in the bedroom. Then, I felt the warmth of the blood in my cheeks rapidly retreat when I heard her say, "How many push-ups did you finally end up doing? Gosh. That was crazy."

I smiled in self-embarrassment. "I think it was one sixty-two. That part of the night is still a little fuzzy."

Sylvia turned on her side and propped up on an elbow. "Tommy couldn't get past one twenty-three," she said. "All you needed to do was a hundred twenty-four to win, but you kept going."

"The whole point was to raise money, right? As long as the cash was flowing, I was going."

"We raised over eleven hundred dollars on that little stunt, which was awesome. Wait... are you saying you could have gone longer?"

I smiled. "No. I was pretty much spent at that point. It was fun. I'm glad I could help."

"What about afterwards?"

"Afterwards?"

"You know, after we came back here and got in the shower."

"I don't have words to describe it."

With a mischievous smile, Sylvia said, "I have one."

I raised my eyebrows, and she lifted the bed sheets to invite me back in. "Yup," she said.

I joined her.

She pushed me on my back and slung a leg over to crawl on top. She wiggled, stretched, and arched her back. Then she lowered herself until we were nose to nose. "Supercalifragilistic."

"Really?"

She nodded.

"Well. I'll take that over *amazing* any day."

"Huh?"

I chuckled. "It's nothing. What time do you have to be at work?"

Biting my ear, she said, "I have a meeting at one."

"Is that going to give us enough time?"

She left my ear and kissed down my neck and worked across my chest. Then she looked up. "If not, I can always reschedule. Now shut up and kiss me. You're wasting precious time."

Four

"You're a son of a bitch. You know that, right?"

"Trust me," I said. "I've been called much worse. I appreciate the lift, though."

"Maybe... deep down... I didn't want to go to work. And it had nothing to do with you. Did that ever cross your mind?"

"I can't recall all the times I didn't want to go to work, but I did. I had little choice."

"We all have choices."

"Sure, but when you're on a ship in the middle of the ocean, and your skipper is expecting you to navigate his vessel across the pond and you don't show up, you have consequences. Serious consequences. If you don't show up for your meeting, what might be your consequences?"

Sylvia ignored my question. She sat behind the wheel of her cobalt blue Jaguar F-Type, arms crossed in feigned defiance, huffing and puffing.

"That's what I thought."

She was beautiful, and the car was fitting for her, but not for me. At six foot three, two hundred twenty pounds, I've sat in more comfortable vehicles. When we arrived, and she shut down the Jag, I opened the door, unfolded my legs, and rolled out on the pavement. I laughed when she looked out the passenger door at me and said, "Really? You got to be kidding me. A muscle man and drama queen wrapped up in one. I can't believe this."

I knelt and changed the subject. Looking at her through the driver's side window, I said, "Thank you for last night."

She turned to look at me and said nothing, but the wry smile that developed on her lips spoke volumes.

"And for this morning," I added.

She reached out and touched my arm. "I should thank you. It's been... well, a long time since..."

I grabbed and held her hand. "I find it difficult to understand how there isn't a permanent man in your life."

In a flash, I watched her transform back to the power-hungry, savvy business professional that took crap from nobody. With a turn of the key, and a revving of the five-hundred seventy-five horses that waited under the hood, she gave me a quick wink and put the car in reverse. "When I can find a man that can handle all this, I might keep him around." After another wink, she reached over and kissed my fingers. After I stood and backed away, she floored the accelerator, dashed away in reverse, then cut the wheel. In another flash, the perfectly executed J-turn had her headed forward. Zero to sixty in about four seconds. I smiled when she sped into the loop to get back on the Overseas Highway and head back to Key West. A one o'clock meeting to close the deal on a four-and-a-half million-dollar ocean-front cottage awaited her presence.

I turned and walked to the front gate of Naval Air Station Key West, on Boca Chica Key. The gate guard looked at my ID. Then the young petty officer said, "Damn, Chief. Excuse me for saying, but she's a pistol."

I read the name on his uniform, laughed, and said, "Swanson. You have no idea, so here's some advice. Stay away from women like her. They will chew you up, spit you out, and when they are done, start all over again."

After a hard swallow, Petty Officer Swanson said, "I think I'd be willing to take my chances."

Walking past and patting him on the back, I said, "I guess I couldn't blame you. Just be careful what you ask for."

"Thanks, Chief."

I held a thumb up in the air.

"Hey, Chief!" Swanson yelled. "Where are you going on foot?"

"To the marina," I said, turning around to walk backward.

"That's a mighty hefty trek out there."

"I don't mind. I could use the exercise."

A charmed life is how I describe my existence. As a U.S. Navy Quartermaster, I served as a ship's navigator on active duty. These days I navigate my vessel, a classic Pearson Vanguard, whenever and wherever I like. I retired as a chief after twenty-three years, and my monthly pension, coupled with a simple and frugal lifestyle, allows me to do pretty much whatever I want. I've met and loved a host of wonderful people. It broke my heart when my best girl ended it all and kicked me to the curb. We were so good together, or at least I thought we were. But she couldn't handle the stresses I placed on our relationship. I get it, but as painful as it was, in a heartbeat I'd do it all over again. Oh, and getting away with murder, I guess you can put that in the charmed column too.

Sylvia Mason was now on my list of folks I've loved. Not a list like putting a notch in a stick or for bragging rights. I don't keep score like that. I don't keep score at all. Sure, throughout my life, there have been one-night stands that meant nothing to me or my partner. Those forgettable faces don't make the list, but the ones that result in a beautiful, meaningful experience do. It wasn't *just* sex, though that's what I had expected. No, once the real Sylvia surfaced, I knew our night would be special. It did not disappoint, and between the moments of erotic passion, we spent long, silent periods in each other's arms. I could tell she appreciated the simple act of being held. So, I did.

Before she got ready for work, we showered together again. Through the steam and sudsy soap lather that we rubbed on each other, we talked about what had happened. She made one thing perfectly clear. There could be no expectations from either of us, but last night couldn't be the only time. "Call me selfish," she said. "I don't care, but when the time is right, I will want you again."

After I agreed, she said, "And one other thing. You must promise to take me sailing on this boat you won't shut up about."

"Twist my arm," I said.

I walked up to the ramp that leads to the docks. I saw *MisChief* resting in her slip. It never ceases to amaze me how stunning she is. Though she is several years older than me, she's always the prettiest girl at the dance. Once I finished admiring my only *real* girl, I took a left and made the short walk to the marina's bar and grill, Navigator's.

Five

Navigator's was enjoying a midday buzz of activity. The place was hopping with sailors: officers and enlisted alike. On duty, titles mean everything. Here, they mean nothing. A sailor is a sailor, from the seaman to an admiral. Okay... admirals and generals may be the exception. If we know either is within our presence, we will extend our respects accordingly. They deserve that much. But if they should come around, you'd never know it. They never make a fuss. Most of the time, everyone is on a first-name basis.

The bar was full of a mix of watermen: anglers, sailing captains, motor cruisers, and your general, run-of-the-mill stinkpotter. I noticed several thirsty folks gathered around the bar. After a quick glance, it was obvious nobody was serving. I looked around for the staff. *Nothing*.

What the hell? If this crowd can't get a drink, a thirsty mutiny will be at hand. I've helped behind the bar before, so

I ducked in and took over. As I went to the sink to wash my hands, I heard someone say, "Where in the hell is Steve?"

I turned my head and answered over my shoulder. "Beats me." I turned around. "Okay. Who is next?" Every hand went up. "Really? Do you want to get served or not?" They kept their hands up, so I took charge and pointed at the closest guy. "Jerry. You're up. Whatcha hav'n?"

It took all of about seven minutes to serve everyone. Most orders were simple. They either wanted bottled beers or pints pulled from the draft station. Most had already started a tab. The rest either paid in cash or started a tab of their own. I handled it all and went about doing what barkeeps do. Wiping down the counter, getting caught up on washing glasses, sweeping the sand up off the floor. When I had the place tidy, I served myself up a glass of Diet Coke, leaned up against the counter, and closed my eyes. Moments later, I heard a familiar voice.

"What in creation are you doing back there?"

I kept my eyes closed. "Your job."

"I wasn't gone that long."

"Yes, you were, so... I clocked in and saved your ass. They wanted your head on a platter." I turned my head toward the voice, opened one eye, and said, "Where have you been, Steve?"

Steve Bailes is another retired chief. He was a signalman, an artist in visual communication: flags, semaphore, flashing light. Steve and I have known each other since I first made landfall here on my way to places not yet known. *MisChief* and I slipped away from Norfolk, Virginia, shortly after my retirement to remove ourselves from an unpleasant situation. It was a dark place and time, and I needed light. I sailed up through the Boca Chica Channel to the base marina, looking for rest, a shower, a stiff drink, and maybe a cheeseburger. Plus, I needed to provision for the next leg of my trip. In many ways, I have Steve to thank for helping me find Port St. Joe, though he never would have known it.

"I had to pick up a package if you have to know." He placed the smiling Amazon box on the bar and joined me.

"So, what do you have there?"

Steve pulled out a pocketknife and cut through the tape. Then, with a goofy smile said, "My sexy Santa suit."

"Sexy, what?"

He opened the box and slung the wads of paper packaging around like a kid at Christmas, which was fitting since the big day was just a couple of weeks away. Then, when he got to the goods, he dragged up the suspendered, fuzzy, red velvet trousers. He held them up against his body. "What do you think?"

I said nothing.

Then he pulled out and slipped on a matching vest trimmed with white, fluffy fur. "You haven't said anything. Whatcha say?"

I reached into the box and pulled out the receipt and product information sheet. It showed a bare-chested Chippendale sporting the vested Santa Muffin outfit. Muscles ripped everywhere, and the suit was tight, leaving very little to the imagination. I looked at the picture, then at Steve. I did this several times until I heard him say, "Well, dammit?"

"I don't know, Steve. Have you given this much thought? I mean, I don't want to sound unsupportive, but do you really think you have the equipment to pull this off?"

"What do you mean?"

I held up the picture. He looked at the muscled hunk and his rippled six-pack, then at his jolly, more realistic Santa belly, then to me. "Screw you, Nigel!"

I couldn't help myself and started laughing.

"Stop it. Stop laughing. Nigel... I'm serious."

I throttled my laughter down to chuckles and said, "I'm sorry, Steve. It's just... just..." I busted out in laughter again and couldn't stop. I finally waved my hand at him and encouraged him between breaths. "Please, put it away. Back in the box. And I promise to stop laughing." I held up three fingers. "Scout's honor."

He did and said, "You're a son of a bitch."

I slowly coughed and pulled myself together. "Thanks. You're the second person to bestow that title on me today."

"Well, they would have been right."

"So, what is all this nonsense about?"

"Nigel, this is your first Christmas in the Keys, right?"

I said nothing.

"It's the SantaCon Pub Crawl. Everybody dresses up in their own version of Santa and we get together, and..."

I interrupted, "And make fools of yourselves."

"You just don't get it. Haven't you learned anything since you've been here? It's all about fun and a good time. If you take yourself too seriously, then you probably should stay home, or better still... find somewhere else to visit or stay." He smiled, slapped on his fat, round belly a few times, and said, "So, to answer your question, this is all the equipment I need."

I couldn't find fitting words for a response, so I just smiled.

"You should play along, too. It will be fun."

"No," I said, "I don't think so. I'll fare better as a casual observer. When does this spectacle, I mean event, happen?"

"This Saturday. We meet up and start the evening off at the Conch Republic Seafood Company, then we roam to the next venue on the schedule."

"I can't wait."

Six

The next couple of days were uneventful. Downright boring by Key West standards, and that was alright with me. I spent a lot of time on *MisChief* doing chores. They are never-ending on a boat. There is always something to do, even more so on a boat a few years away from sixty years old. If you stay ahead of things, it isn't bad. Get behind and you can find yourself overwhelmed. One of the most important parts of a boat to keep your eye on are those parts you can't see when onboard. I'm speaking of the bottom. Especially in a saltwater environment, regular inspections and cleaning are a must to eliminate performance-hampering growth. A bottom ignored and turned over to elements can quickly become fouled and inefficient, or worse.

I was in the water with my hookah rig, a small portable air compressor, hose, and dive regulator. Along with my mask, fins, and weighted belt, it allows me to stay underwater to inspect *MisChief's* bottom and clean away any growth. Luckily, her anti-fouling bottom paint was holding up pretty well and doing its job. There was very little of anything, so a simple brushing did the job.

After I finished cleaning, I swam around, inspected the zinc, the prop, and finally the thru-hulls. As I was about to surface, I heard a loud bong through the hull. Then another. Text messages awaited me in the salon. It was an annoying reminder. Even while lost in the clear, turquoise water of the tropics, civilization still loomed near. *Crap*.

Then, I did more than just think *crap*. I almost did. As I turned to swim for the ladder, I became startled, quickly swam back, and slammed my head on my boat's thick fiberglass layup. "Son of a bitch!" I tried to vocalize through my regulator as I rubbed my noggin. I closed my eyes and let my rapid breathing slow. Then I smiled. A stealthy manatee had snuck up behind me. When I turned, we were face to face. That I wasn't expecting. Despite my brief panicked state, the big sea cow remained stoic and unexcited as it continued to make its advance. I reached out and rubbed its nose and head. "You're a shit. You know that?" I could have sworn it winked at me.

We said our goodbyes. I got out of its way and headed to the surface. On the dock, I took off my gear, grabbed the freshwater hose, and rinsed the salt off everything and me. Then I took refuge to drip dry under the shade canopy stretched above *MisChief's* cockpit. I was almost asleep when I heard a voice. "Did you check my bottom too?"

It was my dock neighbor, Donald Bell. He's a pain in the ass. I tolerate him, because that's what good neighbors do. As a newly retired U.S. Air Force Lieutenant Colonel, my take is he's spoiled and still feels entitled to being served. He thinks he's still on active duty and hasn't yet embraced the retired life. He better, because the crowd around here won't tolerate it for long. His boat is a nice, older model Bertram 35 Flybridge.

I turned my head. "Hey, Don! I gave it a quick gander. There is some growth, but I've seen a lot worse."

"Why didn't you clean it while you were down there?"

"Hey, borrow my hookah dive rig any time you need it."

"But you were just down there. I mean, hell, boy. Where is your initiative?"

"Hey, Donny boy! Don't get fresh with me. I never touch another man's bottom."

"Oh, go to hell," he said, and disappeared back into his salon.

I laughed and tried to go back to sleep, but... BONG!

I went below and grabbed my phone. The messages were all from the same person.

The first. *Good morning!*

The second. *Sunshine.*

The last one. *Hello! Anybody out there?*

Instead of texting back, I hit the call button, and she answered on the second ring.

"Well, there you are, stranger."

I could hear wind noise. "Hey, Sylvia. Got those windows down, huh?"

"You know it. Where have you been?"

"Scaring the shit out of the local manatee population. What's up?"

"Lunch, if you will join me."

I looked at my watch. It was almost 1300. The mention of lunch made me realize I'd eaten nothing since a bagel with my morning coffee. "I am starved. Where?"

"I'm on Stock Island now. Meet me at the Hogfish Grill."

"I still don't have a car."

"Oh, my God! How do you survive without transportation? Can you get to the front gate? I'll come pick you up."

"I think I can manage that. See ya soon."

When Steve pulled through the gate to drop me off, he saw the Jag and the driver that had gotten out to lean against her door and wait. When I said, "Thanks a ton, buddy," and reached for the door, he grabbed my arm.

"What the hell, Nigel. That's Sylvia Mason."

"Yeah? And?"

"That's who's here to pick you up?"

"Yeah, again."

"That's Sylvia Mason."

"I know, and she's waiting. Would you turn loose of my arm? I'm getting hangry."

"But that's Sylvia Mason."

"Would you get a grip, Chief? She's a friend. That's it. Nothing more."

"But that's..."

"Shut up, Steve. That's enough. We're having lunch. Now will you let go?"

I had to jerk my arm out of his grasp. I got out and spoke through Steve's truck window. "Can I rely on you to come back here and pick me up once we're through?"

"Well, yeah."

"Thanks." I turned and headed toward my ride. Steve sat watching. As I got closer, in a hush, I said, "Do me a favor and kiss me for my friend, the voyeur."

She did. When she turned my lips loose, she tossed her keys in the air. When I caught them, she said, "You drive." She walked around the front of the car, but not before turning toward Steve and throwing up a wave.

"You can be evil."

"I've been called worse."

Driving her F-Type should have been fun, but not for me. Finding adequate space behind the wheel was difficult, but I managed. *Thank God it's an automatic.* Shifting would have been impossible. Once we arrived at the restaurant, the next biggest challenge was getting out without looking like a fool. No such luck. I ended up rolling out with my back toward the pavement. Using my hands, I crab-crawled away out of the cockpit. Free of the Jag, I stood up quickly, only to be met with a round of applause from several laughing onlookers. I sent them back a celebrity wave. I looked at Sylvia. "You did this on purpose."

She walked around and took me by the hand. "And you are a good sport."

She had arranged for the staff to reserve us an outside table overlooking the marina and boats. She had their famous Hogfish sandwich with fries, and she washed it all down with two glasses of Pinot Grigio. I had the Ceasar salad with blackened scallops and club soda with lime.

"You order and eat like a girl," she said.

"I eat like a guy that once didn't care about anything and let himself go. I gained a ton of weight. That was right before I sailed down here. I made a promise to myself. Never again. Had you met the old Nigel at the Green Parrot, you wouldn't have given him the time of day."

"You make me sound shallow."

"No, it's just the truth. I wasn't very attractive, and I damn sure couldn't have done all those push-ups. I wouldn't have even offered to do them."

She reached over and grabbed my hand. "I don't believe it for a minute."

"Well, it doesn't matter now. Thanks to eating and drinking right, I'm back to fighting weight where I need to be."

"Why is that?"

I looked at my plate and loaded my fork with salad and scallops. "Because sometimes, my life depends upon it."

I closed my eyes tight and thought, *Nigel. You're an idiot. Why did you say that?* I opened my eyes and found her strange and confused glare. "I'm sorry," I said. "That was a stupid thing to say. I sound crazy."

She said nothing, and I tried to lighten the mood. "Hey, look at it this way. Had I not lost all that weight, there wouldn't have been any way my fat ass could have gotten in your car."

I laughed at myself.

She didn't, but said, "I think you know me well enough by now that I wouldn't judge you. And, yes, it may have been a stupid thing to say, but I'd guess you're being more truthful than you let on."

I said nothing.

She took a drink from her wineglass and said, "And it doesn't scare me a lick."

I said nothing. *Maybe it should.*

She changed the subject. "So, how is your lunch?"

"Exceptional. Thank you for the invite."

"My pleasure. I enjoy your company."

"I enjoy yours too," I said, reaching over to grab her hand.

We exchanged quiet stares for a spell until I excused myself. "I need to run to the head."

That was the excuse I gave, and after all the water I drank, it would probably be a smart visit. But I wanted to run down Tony, our server, so I could pay the bill. I found him delivering a drink order at the bar. When I told him what I wanted, he shook his head no.

"Are you wanting to piss off the lady?" he asked.

"No. Of course not. I just wanted to settle. That's all."

"Well, she's already taken care of everything."

"Damn," I mumbled.

"I'll tell you one other thing. She eats lunch here almost every day. Sits at the same table and has two glasses of wine with whatever she orders. This is the first time in probably a year and a half that I've seen her invite anybody to dine with her. You must be special."

I looked over my shoulder and found Sylvia sipping her wine and looking out over the water. I thanked Tony and walked back to the table and sat down. She turned toward me and said, "Sorry. Beat you to it. My treat."

"Well, thank you. I'm not accustomed to having beautiful women buy my meals."

She laughed. "You're welcome. And besides, you're a cheap date."

I rolled my eyes.

"So," she said, "what are you going to do with the rest of the day?"

"I don't know. Folks at the marina are decorating their boats for the lighted boat parade. I was thinking of putting on some trailer trash lights on *MisChief* and joining in. I've had a friend hint that if I don't go with the *fun flow* around here, I might get my ass run off."

She laughed. "We have those types around. Most of them work little and are broke most of the time. So, are you going to do it?"

"Do what?"

"The boat parade, silly. I'd love to come along if there's room."

"Sylvia, *MisChief* is a 32-footer. I imagine there will be far larger and more grandiose boats for you to jump on."

She scrunched her eyebrows. "That's twice in less than one hour that you've hinted that I'm shallow."

"I'm sorry. It's just you are…"

Now she had her eyebrows lifted and arched.

"Okay. I'll shut up now. Not another word." I pinched my fingers and pretended to zip my lips shut.

"So, is that a yes?"

"*MisChief* and I would love to have you aboard. I think it's this Friday night, if your calendar is clear."

"If it isn't, I'll clear it."

"Perfect."

As we left the restaurant and walked toward the car, a ruckus between two watermen developed on the docks. Sylvia and I stopped to look. One guy held a wooden oar, ready to swing. The other brandished a short baseball bat.

Sylvia clutched at my arm and said, "Damn. I just took a chill. Let's go, asshole."

I looked down at her face. It looked mad and hateful.

"Do what? Asshole?"

"Screw you," she said. "Catch your own ride home."

She shoved me away and headed toward her car. With amazement, I witnessed a turn in attitude that floored me and left me confused. I yelled, "What did I do?" She didn't look back but answered with a middle finger.

"What are you? Freak'n bipolar or something?"

Now her finger was higher in the air and shaking violently.

Dammit. I wish I hadn't said that. I turned my attention back toward the argument on the dock. Others had joined the fray. I ran down amongst them and placed myself between the two guys. I used my right hand to shove the chest of "Batman," and my left to push back the guy with the oar. "What the hell is going on here?"

The guy with the oar barked, "He started it!"

The guy with the bat charged, screaming, "Bullshit! You did!"

I planted a powerful, right overhanded fist to his nose. He went backward, down on the dock like he had been clotheslined. I spun around in time to see the oar being raised. He was going to clobber the other guy while he was out cold.

"Whoa! Whoa! Stop!" But he didn't, so before he could come down with the oar, I drove my fist into his gut. I felt his soft tissue give and my knuckles seemed to drive past his liver. He let go of the oar and it fell behind him as he leaned forward and puked on the dock. "Would everybody just calm down, dammit!"

Behind the guy that I laid out cold, three other people were arguing, saying hateful things to each other and making no sense. I turned around, and the same was happening down at the other end of the dock. Everybody was mad. *What the hell was going on?* I turned round and round, taking in the commotion. Then I took a few steps back toward the restaurant and could hear feuds and quarreling coming from inside. "What the..."

Then I heard laughter. I turned around, and that's where I saw him or it, actually. It was the guy in the man goat costume, looking more real than he did the other night at the Green Parrot. He stood, cackling away in the brush line on the other side of Front Street. "Hey, you!" I took a few steps, but before I could even get to the street, I got whacked in the back of the head and went to my knees. "Damn!"

Jumping to my feet, I was ready to fight. I saw my sucker-punching adversary and prepared a punishing blow but stopped cold. It was an old man, probably well on his way to ninety. *What is the matter with you?* He held his cane at the ready, and I put up my hands, backing away. "Okay, Pops. You win. There is no fight here." He scowled at me and turned around. Rubbing the back of my head, I looked across the street. The goatman was gone.

Seven

I called an Uber to get me back to the naval air station. I sat outside the pass office to wait for Steve to pick me up. He said that he would be a few minutes, but when a *few* turned into *several*, I got up and started walking. At about the half-way point down Midway Avenue, Steve's truck came into sight. I crossed the street and waited. Steve stopped, and I got in.

"Sorry it took so long. I had deliveries and I couldn't leave the vendors, plus they never move very quickly to begin with."

"No problem," I said. "I needed to do some thinking, anyway. Walking helps."

"How did your lunch go?"

"Fine." I lied. My phone never bonged, but I checked it anyway to see if Sylvia had returned any of the three texts that I had sent her. She didn't.

"You look troubled, Nige."

"I'm good. Just tired."

"It's been killing me. How is it you know Sylvia Mason? I mean damn, man. She's like the richest woman in the Keys. And single!"

"I know, Steve. I know. The Green Parrot is where I met her. Now we're friends." *Or at least I thought we were.*

"Man, that is one hell of a catch."

"There is no catch, Steve. And if you don't mind, we both enjoy our privacy, so please don't go making a big deal" I watched him turn his head and cut his eyes at me. "Oh, crap! How many people have you already told?"

"Well... I don't know. Several of the fellas were in the bar."

"Just forget it," I said. "Whatever. I don't need to hear anymore. It is what it is."

"But man, she put that lip lock on you. I saw it."

I held up my hand. "It's alright. It's okay, Steve. She's just a friend, and that is my story."

Steve dropped the subject and didn't bring up another. I was thankful. When he stopped his truck at the docks, he asked, "You coming by later for an afternoon soda?"

"Yeah. I probably will, might even dip a bit into the Woodford Reserve. It's been that kind of day."

Since arriving in Key West, I may have gotten into the spirits two or three other times. Times of weakness are what I like to call them. It wasn't pretty. I am human, after all.

When I got back to *MisChief*, I sat in the cockpit to get comfortable and think about the bizarre incidents that unfolded at the restaurant. One thing was certain: nothing about it felt natural or organic. The widespread anger and general pissy moods puzzled me. Especially the way Sylvia turned on me. It was genuine anger. I could see it in her eyes.

After a while, I verbalized a decision, so I could hear it with my own ears, "You know what? I don't give a shit! None of it has anything to do with me. I did nothing to deserve the treatment Sylvia gave me, and I should have let those dock jockeys kill each other. It wouldn't have been any skin off my back. All it got me was a knot on the head by some old coot. Mind your own business from now on, Nigel!" I rubbed the knot given to me by the old fart. "You're an idiot!"

"You alright, boy? Who you talk'n to like that?"

I turned my head. Don Bell stood on the dock, looking down at me. A judgmental gaze about his eyes.

I said nothing.

"Do you need a mental hospital or a padded room?"

"I might, if things keep going like they are."

He grunted and said, "That doesn't sound encouraging. Just don't go psycho on me. I don't need some whacked-out crazy-ass squid as a neighbor."

"Trust me. If I go psycho on you, you will know it. Have you ever seen bat-shit crazy?"

He said nothing.

"Well, you're looking at it."

He walked away, saying, "Just keep your ass in check."

I raised my voice to follow him. "Can't make you any promises, and you can always request a new slip. I was here first."

My voice must have carried. From somewhere in the marina, someone said, "You can keep him, Nigel. We don't want him over here."

Eight

It was late Friday afternoon. I sat beneath one of the thatched tiki huts, sipping ice water and watching all the activity in the marina. People scurried around, making final preparations for the lighted boat parade. The lights I had ordered online for *MisChief* remained in the smiling Amazon box they arrived in. I would return them on Monday.

From inside Navigator's, I heard Steve yell. "Hey, Nigel. You gonna be here for a while?"

He stood at the door, phone in his hand, palm covering the mouthpiece. "Yeah! Not going anywhere. Who wants to know?"

"The Old Man!"

"The skipper? Right!" I laughed. "Am I being recalled to active duty? Tell him I'm ready to go."

I watched him say something into the phone and cover the mouthpiece again. "He said, 'No way. You're damaged goods.'"

"That is an understatement. Really... who are you talking with?"

"Nobody, just messing with you. Can I get you another Dasani on ice?"

I shook my glass. It was half full. "I'm okay for now. Check on me later. Thanks."

Time passed by, and I sipped easily at my leisure. It was shaping up to be another beautiful Key West evening. The sky was clear and dry. The December temps were not angry at seventy-three. It was going to be perfect. My watch reported 1713. The sun was dropping fast, and as darkness slowly took over, the lights of the boats shined brighter. They would be leaving soon. They had plenty of time but needed to get to Schooner Wharf. The parade starts at 2200.

From over my shoulder, a fresh glass of ice and a bottle of water got placed in front of me.

"Thanks," I said, as I watched the first of the boats pull out of their slips. Then a marble wine chiller containing a bottle of pinot grigio came next.

"Hey," I said, turning. "I didn't..." Then I turned back to watch the departures.

"I thought we were going to do the parade?"

I said, "Changed my mind. I'm the skipper. I can do that."

She walked around to face me and block my view. She had her hands behind her back.

"Excuse me. You make a better door than a window."

"Very original," she said.

"I'm sorry, it's all I have."

"I have something."

"What?"

She pulled her hands around. Her fingers clutched a floppy straw hat. I looked from the hat to her more than twice.

"I'm so sorry. I don't know what got into me."

"I tried to text you, Sylvia. I tried to call... and nothing."

"I was mad, dammit!"

"About what? Answer that for me."

She sat next to me. "I don't know. That's the problem. I was angry for like three days. Hell, I was mad at everybody. It made no sense."

"Ya think?"

"Nigel, please. I'm trying to apologize."

She was. Her words were sincere and her expression honest. I'm probably one of the few that have seen that side of her, yet there I was, being a prick. I held out my hand, and she took it. "I'm sorry. You were the last person I expected to see out..." I stopped to think. "Wait, how did you get on base?"

She returned a smile.

I turned to look at the bar. Steve stood in the breezeway, leaning up against the door frame, arms crossed, a shit-eating grin stretched across his face.

"Did Steve go get you?"

"No, I think you guys call it the duty driver."

I closed my eyes, thinking about Steve's earlier phone call. "Oh, let me guess. You know the skipper, and you called his office."

"We've met at more than a few socials and fundraisers." Then she hugged me. "Will you forgive me?"

I hugged her back. "I don't know what you are talking about. Now pour yourself a glass of wine and let's watch our own private lighted boat parade."

As she poured, I stood and faced Steve. Placing my hands together in front of my belt, Steve stopped holding the door up and did the same. Then I started moving my hands around, pointing this way and that. When I finished, I brought my hands back down and together.

"What the heck are you doing?" she asked.

I nodded my head at Steve.

She turned to see him carrying on similarly. "Would you please explain what is going on?"

I sat back down. "I was ordering a drink. Steve's an old signalman and I've been practicing my semaphore. That's sign language for sailors."

Moments later, Steve brought out a glass and set it down. "Here's your bourbon, brother. You signaled *Woodward* Reserve, not *Woodford*. And *meet* instead of *neat*, but I knew what you meant."

"Thank you, brother."

He turned toward Sylvia. "Is there anything I can get for the lady?"

She grabbed hold of my arm and said, "No. I think I have everything I need right here."

"Very well, Miss." Then he looked at me and said, "Just a friend, huh?"

"Thanks, Steve. That will be all."

Darkness fell, and the lighted boats were fully underway, lining up for the channel. Sylvia and I found a couple of empty Adirondacks and pulled them out by the water for a better view. We counted fourteen boats in all. They were pretty to see as they eased by.

Looking out over the water, I said, "Isn't this better?"

She reached over and kissed my cheek.

I turned and returned a soft kiss to her lips. "Thank you for coming."

She settled back into her chair and said, "Thanks for letting me stay."

"It was a tough decision."

She slapped my arm. *Whack!*

Nine

Midnight approached, and we still sat out by the water chit-chatting. A few of the boats returned from the parade. Some kept the celebration alive. For two boats, things must not have gone well. Heated conversations and a healthy dose of the blame game were being tossed about between the skippers and crews.

"Damn," I said. "Something must have gone to crap."

"Know how they feel."

I turned my head.

"I'm out of wine."

"And the bar's closed."

I turned my head to look back at Navigator's. The light was still on, and Steve's truck was still in the lot.

"Well, maybe not. It looks like Steve is still around. I'm sure I could get you something. What will it be?"

I went to stand, but she grabbed my arm. "No. I was just kidding. It's late and I need to get going."

Throughout the night, I never once offered that she should stay the night on *MisChief*, nor did she hint that she'd like to. If she had thought about it, I was glad she had said nothing. I didn't want to have to decline the notion. It wasn't something I needed or wanted, and I could sense the same from her.

"That may be a problem. Your car is at the gate, and I don't..."

"Have a car. I forgot."

"And it wouldn't be cool to wake the duty driver for something like this. Though we could."

"No. No. Don't do that."

I stood and reached out with my hand. "Come on. I'm sure Steve won't mind giving up his truck for a few minutes."

We walked over to the door. It was still open, and I was about to go in, but I jumped back to look at Sylvia.

"What are you grinning at?" she asked.

I nudged my head toward the door. "Look. Try not to let him see you."

She moved past me and peeked in through the door and immediately covered her smile with her fingers. I joined her and watched over her shoulder. Then I whispered in her ear. "That's the marina's sexy Santa."

She laughed and swung her free hand and slapped my leg. "Stop it."

Steve was modeling his sexy Santa suit for himself in the mirror. With no shirt, his hairy belly kept the front of the red velvet vest from closing, and he didn't seem to care. He tried different poses and stances. When he turned around, we jumped back, and I knocked over a trash can. When we heard Steve yell, wanting to know who was here, we exchanged *Oh Shit* looks and laughter.

We put our backs to the wall, and I raised my voice. "Ah! It's me, Steve. Nigel. Sorry about that. I ran into something."

Steve came barging outside and saw the trash scattered. "Damn, Nigel."

Sylvia ducked in behind me to hide and giggle. "I know. My fault. I'll clean it up."

He put his fists on his hips and his belly poked out of the vest even further. "Damn right you will."

I laughed.

"What's so damn funny?"

"Nothing. Really." I pulled myself together. "Listen. I need your truck for a few minutes. I need to run Ms. Mason back to the gate. Do you mind?"

Sylvia slid out from behind me. "I'd appreciate it… Santa."

"Huh?" He had forgotten that he had the costume on. Remembering, he said, "Oh! Yeah." He pranced and spun around. "Do you like it?"

She said, "I love it."

He picked at the back of the trousers. "I wish there was a little more room in the seat."

I burst out laughing. "Maybe… the seat is fine, and you just need a little less ass."

Sylvia stepped away to look at me. "Nigel! You're being mean and cruel!"

"No, I'm not. I'm just poking the bear."

"And this *bear* has a truck that you need."

I said, "Oh, yeah."

"That's what I thought. Fat chance now, bucko."

"Oh, Steve. Knock it off. I was just..."

Sylvia stepped up. "Yes, we do. I do." She cut me a quick look. *Shut up.* "Steve, please ignore him. I need to get home and it's a mighty long walk to the highway."

Steve grumbled and finally went back inside. He brought out the keys and threw them at me. They bounced off my chest. "Hey! You could have taken an eye out!"

"Hey, nothing!" he said. "I'm only doing this for the lady. Now get out of here and get your butt back to clean this mess up."

On the ride back to the gate, she asked, "So, if I had to guess, that's Steve's SantaCon outfit?"

"Yeah. Pretty ridiculous, huh?"

"Honey, have you ever been to a Key West SantaCon?"

"No."

She laughed and said, "You haven't seen anything... yet. Are you dressing up and going?"

"Going? I had planned to. Dressing up? Not my style. Are you going?"

"I dress for SantaCon every year. It's fun."

At the gate, I ran around, opened her door, and walked her to the car. When she unlocked the car with her fob, I opened her door. "Thank you for coming. I had a really enjoyable time."

She pulled up close and wrapped her arms around me. "Me too. It was perfect."

I pulled her into a long goodnight kiss. She didn't complain, but when we finished, she said, "Buy a car, dammit! Or a bicycle built for two or something, for crying out loud."

Ten

I woke up to complete darkness and Sylvia's scent. *Did I go to bed alone or not? Could have sworn that I did.* I put my hand out just to make sure. The spot where she would have been was vacant. I was alone, and it left me feeling empty. The evening had confirmed one thing for me. I liked her company.

The shirt I wore the night before lay wadded up next to me. I grabbed it and brought it to my nose. There she was.

She demanded I dance with her whenever a favorite song came on, and she shot down my persistent attempts to decline every time. I finally just gave up. It was hopeless. Plus... I was having fun. Luckily, all the songs were slow. Almost anybody, even Nigel Logan, can dance to a slow song and not look too foolish. By the fourth song, she had me gently swinging her around. It was a fun night, and it left me with nice memories and a Columbia fishing shirt holding the subtle, classic remnants of her Chanel No. 5.

I swung my feet around and climbed out of the v-berth. After splashing my face with some water from the sink in the head, I put on water for coffee. Then, like every other morning when it's not raining, I open the hatch, make my way to the dock, walk out to the end, spread my feet apart, place my hands on my hips, and water the ducks. It makes no sense to fill up the holding tank if I can avoid it.

It never bothers me to walk around the docks naked. I never even look around to make sure the coast is clear. Why would I? Who else, other than me, is up and moving at four something in the morning? Very few, if anybody.

While I waited for the water to boil, I grabbed my phone from where I laid it the day before to charge. It lay face down, and when I picked it up, its notification light blinked. There were three text messages. They all came in close succession. I saw the sender's name, and I smiled: Trixie. The wife of my whacked-out crazy buddy Red. I opened the first one and my smile grew even larger. It was a simple picture of my old dog, Daisy. She's my old girlfriend's dog now. Daisy was curled up under my favorite bar stool—number seventeen—at the City Bar in Port St. Joe.

The next text was another picture that made me laugh out loud. It was the entire gang, my Forgotten Coast Family, bunched up together in front of the bar: Red, Trixie, Luke, Maxine, Daisy, Brian Bowen, Luther (Little Bit) Collins, and Joe Crow. Two pretty barkeeps, Tracy and Tara, were behind the bar and standing on something to be included in the shot. The one person who wasn't in the picture was Candice, the bar manager, and my once singular love interest. She wasn't in the picture for probably two reasons. First, she's the one that probably took the picture, and second, she didn't want to be in it.

The third text was only three words. *We miss you!*

I texted back. *You made me smile and laugh. I miss all of you too!*

The Fly Away Cafe was the local grill at the marina and located right next to Navigator's. They didn't open until 1000, but I got there a little early and took a seat at a table under one of the Tiki huts. At 0945, I saw one of the wait staff unlock and open the door.

"Might as well come on in," she said. "Diet Coke?"

I got up and walked toward the door. "Yes. And the usual."

"Three egg veggie omelet. Hold the taters. Got it."

She held the door for me, and I kissed her cheek as I passed. "Thanks, Lisa."

"No problem." She locked the door. "It will be a few minutes, though. The kitchen is still doing food prep."

"All good."

I sat at my usual table, and Lisa brought my diet soda. They had the radio up loud. Pirate Radio. WKYZ 101.7 on the FM dial. Sheryl Crow belted out "If It Makes You Happy" as the staff danced, getting the room ready to open.

At 1000, three things happened. Lisa turned the volume of the radio down from blaring to comfortable listening, unlocked the door, and the Saturday morning disk jockey started his radio show. Before then, automation took care of all the music and commercial programing.

After thanking everybody for tuning in, he did the weather and marine report, then went into some local news. The first thing he spoke of was the chaos that erupted along the waterfront at the lighted boat parade. There had been scattered fights, disorderly conduct, and a bit of vandalism. They arrested eleven people on various charges and hauled them off to jail. "What the hell, folks?" he said on air. "Have you all lost your freaking minds? It's Christmas. Act like it!" He paused for a beat and continued, "So much for the news. Here's some Jimmy Buffett Christmas music. Maybe that will put some of you in a better mood."

As "Ho Ho Ho and a Bottle of Rum" started, Lisa brought my omelet.

"Hey, Lisa. Did you go to the boat parade last night?"

"No, but I heard what happened. It was crazy. My old boyfriend was one of the guys that got arrested. He's a prick, but he's not stupid enough to punch a cop. At least I didn't think so."

"He punched a cop? Not smart."

"That's what a friend told me. She said, 'Todd,' that's his name, 'just kept coming until he got tased.'"

"Ouch. I got tased once. It's no fun."

Lisa jumped back, surprised. "You? You've been tased?"

"Long story. Happened a few years ago. I was choking the shit out of a guy, trying to kill him, and the cops stepped in and spoiled my fun."

Lisa stood there with her mouth wide open, then she pulled back into a smile and waved her hand at me. "Mr. Logan! You are so full of it." She went back to work, mumbling. "Got tased trying to kill somebody. Yeah, right?"

Eleven

I got to Conch Republic Seafood early, or so I thought. Steve said the SantaCon festivities kicked off at 1800, but several folks had gotten a head start, especially with the drinking. I immediately identified a handful of Santas that were in no condition to make it to the starting line. If they couldn't grab a ride home soon, they would find a gutter somewhere to sleep it off.

I saddled up on stool 17 and ordered a dozen raw oysters from the bar to start things off. Then followed it up with a catch-of-day sandwich, fresh grouper. I had it blackened. Hold the fries. The bartender seemed a little disappointed when I ordered club soda with lime, but he got over it when I slipped him a twenty and said, "Here. This is for you."

The oysters were not as salty as I'm used to, but the sandwich and fish were prepared perfectly. I pushed my plate forward, and the bartender came by and recharged my glass. The place was hopping with Santas, so I turned my stool around to people watch. It wasn't even six yet, and every imaginable type of Santa roamed the establishment. Sylvia was right. Steve's sexy Santa get-up would be boring compared to what I had already seen. There were plenty of Santas adorned with traditional garb. Some of them looked very convincing. But in the mix were more than a few pirate and Rastafarian Santas. There was at least one Grinch Santa, and one gaggle of guys wore only Ho-Ho hats and red G-Strings trimmed out in white fur. There was even an Elvis Santa. The women were fantastic. Those that could pull off a sexy Mrs. Claus did not disappoint; the drag queens trying to pull off the same couldn't come close. The fishnet stockings, black stiletto heels, and hairy cleavage did nothing for me. Thank God.

My favorite Santa was a sexy Playboy Bunny Santa. There were several of them together, but one captured my full attention. When she caught me staring, she and her group started through the crowd toward me. She moved with ease, gliding through the holiday traffic. When she got to me, she took her hands and parted my knees to move in closer. She ran her fingers through my hair, then pulled me into a long kiss. When we came up for air, I said, "Hello, Sylvia."

She backed away and spun around a couple of times. "What do you think?"

"I think you win the party. Hefner would have been proud. Can I buy you a drink?"

"A glass of pinot grigio would be nice. Thank you."

I got the bartender's attention and ordered. He made quick work of it and came back, reaching over the bar. "Here ya go, Ms. Sylvia."

She took the glass. "Thank you, darling."

He walked away, and I said, "Do you know all the bartenders in this town?"

She slapped my arm. "No. Don't be silly. They all know me."

"I can see that."

She placed her free hand on my cheek. "Don't think of me as rude. I hate to drink and run, but the ladies and I need to mingle."

I smiled, and before leaving, she gave my face a gentle pat.

Ah, I thought. *The public Sylvia had returned. Strong-minded. Powerful. Savvy. In control.* As she moved away, I said, "That's one hell of an act you got going on there."

She turned and returned a playful wink.

The guy sitting next to me grabbed my arm. He was drunk. "Damn! Do you... know her?"

"Nope. She's just a kisser. She'll kiss anybody."

He looked at me. "Whaaaat?"

I provided a confirmed nod, and he jumped to make chase. "Hey! Bunny! I like... bunnies." His pursuit lasted about four steps before he planted his face on the floor.

I winced and watched as the bouncers dragged him off to the side.

The empty stool didn't stay vacant long. A skinny elderly looking rascal mounted it. He looked at me and nodded while pulling on the end of his wide-brimmed hat. Long stringy grey hair hung out the back of his headgear. He had bushy eyebrows and a long goatee to match his hair. No moustache. I nodded back. He wore a weathered white shirt under a faded red vest trimmed with faded gold edges, yellow stockings, and black leather slippers.

He said, "They all look ridiculous. Wouldn't you agree?"

I looked him square in the eye and did my best not to snicker. "I'm not sure how to answer that. Some of them certainly got a little creative." Then I pointed. "But look at that one. He looks like the genuine article. There's no telling how much he paid for that suit."

"Seventeen hundred twenty-seven dollars and thirty-two cents."

I scrunched my eyebrows. "Huh?"

"It's how much he paid. Waste of money."

"Do you know him?"

He turned and looked at me. A tiny flash came from his eyes, and with a convincing voice of honesty, he said, "I know everybody, Nigel." Then he returned his gaze to the crowd.

I almost asked how he knew my name but didn't. There was a kind sincerity in his voice that caused me to accept his explanation. I put my hand out and said, "I'm sorry, but you have me at a disadvantage."

He took my hand and said, "Kris. With a K."

"Glad to meet you."

"It's good knowing you."

Knowing?

"Why do you say the guy wasted his money?"

"Because that isn't what Sinterklaas looks like."

"Sinter what?"

"Sinterklaas. It's a nickname derived from Sint Nikolas. That's Dutch for Saint Nicholas."

I shook my head. *What?*

"The world's current depiction of your *Santa Claus* is partially based on the poem by Clement Clarke Moore, "An Account of a Visit from Saint Nicholas.""

"Never heard of it."

"That's because you know it as 'Twas the Night Before Christmas."

"What are you saying?"

"The poem. It's a lie. All of it. Perhaps lie is too strong a word. Fabrication. That's better."

I said nothing.

"He wrote it to entertain his three daughters. When he published it, he did so for fun. Not as a fact. The poem's popularity grew rapidly and in no time the words were being read to most every child in the world."

"And if you tell a lie often enough," I said.

"Exactly. It becomes the truth. Reality." He paused for a few beats. "Several decades later, a cartoonist named Thomas Nast took the poem's description of the *right jolly old elf* and drew the first image of..." He pointed at one of the better Santas and continued, "...your modern-day Santa. In his cartoons, he also extended the lie... I mean, fabrication. He added the elves, the workshop, the North Pole, and Ms. Claus."

"What?" I said. "No wife? No Mrs. Claus?"

"I never married."

"What's your last name?"

He turned to me, and the twinkling flash returned. "Kringle."

Twelve

"Kringle? As in Kris Kringle? As in... Santa Claus?"

With another flash from his eyes, he nodded. "The genuine article. As you would say. And for the record, I prefer Sinter over Santa."

Okay, I thought. *What am I supposed to do with this?* "And you say there is no North Pole."

"Oh, there's a North Pole..."

I felt stupid.

"...there's just no elves building toys in some silly workshop up there."

"Okay. If there is no North Pole, where is home?"

"A town in Turkey. Myra."

In an instant, he changed the subject to refocus on the crowd. "They all look silly, but they're happy. I'll give you that." Then he pointed. "Your buddy over there. He's mighty confident to be wearing that outfit."

I looked to where he pointed. It was Steve. He was dancing with some gals that were dressed as elves. "You know Steve? How did you know..."

He turned toward me and hit me with another twinkle.

"Those guys over there," he said. "They're nothing more than leftovers from the Hemingway look-alike contest in red coats." He lowered and shook his head. "Poor Ernest. He was given a raw deal."

"Mental illness and suicide," I said, "are never pretty."

The old man's head snapped toward me and said, "Suicide? There was no suicide. That's just what *they* told everyone. He didn't shoot himself."

"What are you talking about? It's a well-known fact that he took his own life."

"A well-known fact, huh? You mean like I'm supposed to look like them," he said, pointing to the crowd.

"So, if it wasn't suicide, then how?"

"Assassination."

"What?... Who?"

"Your government. The CIA. When everybody thought he was going crazy with schizophrenia and paranoia, turns out he was right, and they were wrong."

"If what you say is true, why?"

"It's not important now, but he knew things that your government didn't want to get out."

"That's crazy," I said.

"Is it, huh? You were in the Navy. Are you telling..."

"Stop! Stop right there, old man! How do you know this stuff? Just who in the hell are you?"

"Please. Call me Sinter. I told you. I'm Sinterklaas, a lover of God and the Christ child, the patron saint of children, sailors, and the poor. I was a monk and until my death, I dedicated my life to helping the needy, the sick, and the suffering."

I felt my eyes grow wide. "Your death, you say. And when was this... Sinter?"

"December 6th. Around AD 343."

"After Death... 343?"

He slowly nodded.

Okay. This guy has a screw loose.

"It became to be known as Saint Nicholas Day and parents of children used this day to continue my tradition of secretly providing gifts and treats to well-behaved children."

"So at least the part about being naughty or nice is correct. Did you go down the chimneys?"

"You could say that, yes. But no chimneys. I told you. That was all a... fabrication."

This is rich, Key West crazy rich. "So, if the day of gift giving is on December 6th, why is it done on December 25th?"

"Well, I don't know how *rich* it is, but..."

Did the man just read my mind?

"...it's a long story. Basically, you have Martin Luther to thank for that. Many, including Martin Luther, wanted to do away with Saint Nicholas Day altogether. The day had become so popular, it became viewed as blasphemous and took away from the focus of Christianity." He paused for a few beats and a tear appeared in his eye. "Funny, huh? How history repeats itself." After flicking the tear away, he continued, "Anyway, the reverend wanted to save the principle of gift-giving to children. So, they moved gifting to December 25th, intending to represent the gifts that Christ gives to humanity."

"Why are you telling me all this?"

"To begin with, you asked. More importantly, I know you to be a believer."

"Me? A believer?"

"Yes. Like your friend, Randy. You both have shirts professing your beliefs. You both believe in things others can't comprehend."

"Randy? You mean, Red? How do you know about that?"

He answered with a slow close and opening of his eyes with another twinkle. *Dang!*

The shirts he mentioned have two words on the front. *I Believe*. Above that is the silhouette of Bigfoot. Red's belief in Bigfoot—he prefers to call it a Yeti—is based strictly on faith. He has never seen the beast. I, on the other hand, have had the unpleasant experience of standing toe to toe with the creature.

"Tell me! How do you know about…"

A commotion erupting from outside interrupted me. Loud arguing, followed by ear-piercing screams, caused me and Sinter to look toward the streets.

"What the hell is going on?"

He looked at me and said, "He's here?"

"Who's here?"

"Krampus! I have to go."

He jumped off his stool and ran. I was close behind. When we got to the curb, I stopped. He kept going. The parking lot and streets were in a state of mayhem: fist fights, scuffling, and arguments consumed the party-goers. Then I saw it. The half-man, half-goat looking character was on the other side of the street.

When it saw Sinter charging, it took off down Elizabeth Street. I took off and followed. The old man was fast, faster than I would have imagined, and he continued his pursuit around the corner at Dey Street. As I made the turn, I slowed to a stop, then walked looking around. They were gone. I ran my fingers through my hair. "What in the world is going on?"

Thirteen

I stood in a stupor. *How could they have vanished like that? I wasn't that far behind.*

I could still hear the screams and hollering back at Conch Republic. Then a thought crossed my mind: *Sylvia*. I took off in a dash to get back.

The place was crazy, but maybe only a quarter of the folks remained. The smart people got out fast; the rest remained. All in some sort of uproar. The cops were outnumbered, but they did their best to restore order.

As I entered the crowd to look for her, the corner of my eye caught a guy coming at me fast. I turned to face him and ducked under his swinging, balled-up fist. I stepped to the side as his momentum carried him past me, exposing his right kidney. I landed two powerful blows to the bullseye. When he straightened up, arching his back in pain, I landed a rabbit punch that sent him to the ground. I wasn't in the mood for a fair fight.

I moved through the crowd, pushing and slinging people to the side as I called out for her. No answer. Another guy wanted to fight. He was much smaller than me. As he came running, a stiff arm to his forehead sent him down to the pavement. I stepped over him. "Damn, you people. Knock it off."

Then I saw Sylvia. She was in the middle of the parking lot, struggling with some guy dressed as a bad Santa. He was behind her and had his arms around her waist. He kept trying to pull her away, but she fought back hard. Madder than hell. The look on her face actually made me grin. Then I took off running.

"Put her down, pal. I'm warning you."

He didn't. I'm not even sure he heard me. When I got there, he was dragging her away while she flailed around.

"Dude! Did you hear me? Put her down."

He ignored me. Didn't even look at or acknowledge me. I took up a position behind him and gave one last warning. "This is it, buddy. Drop her now."

He didn't, so I took my palms and played his ears like a set of marching band cymbals. He turned her loose, and I popped his ears again, even harder. To his knees he went, and I pushed him on over with the heel of my shoe, saying, "I bet you heard that, asshole."

I looked up and saw Sylvia walking away, moving fast. I caught up with her.

"Are you okay?"

"Leave me alone, jerk."

"Sylvia! Slow down. It's me."

She kept going, so I grabbed her by the arm and turned her toward me. "We have got to get…"

WHACK!

She smacked the crap out of my face, but I maintained my grip, trying not to hurt her. She went to hit me again but stopped mid-swing. Her eyes met mine.

"It's me, Sylvia. Nigel."

I watched as her eyes fluttered. Then she collapsed. I caught her before she hit the ground, but the clutch purse she carried fell to the pavement. With her in my arms, I leaned over, picked it up, opened it, and found her key fob. "Now, where exactly did you park that sardine can?" I pushed the alarm button.

BEEP! BEEP! BEEP! BEEP!

I looked around. It was on Green Street. I shut off the alarm and lifted Sylvia into my arms.

Once I got her in the passenger seat and buckled her in, I moved the driver's seat back and crammed my body and butt behind the wheel. I just wanted to get us out of there. I fired up the Jag and took off down Green Street to put some distance between us and the chaos. I took a left on Whitehead and looked for a good place to park. The lot at the La Concha Hotel looked as good as any place.

I found a spot, shut down the engine, and sat with my eyes closed to catch my breath. I tilted my head to look at Sylvia. She was still out cold. "Where do we go from here, darling?"

I needed her home address, and I didn't want to root through her purse unless I had to. I opened the glove box looking for registration or insurance papers that might point me in the right direction. No good. Everything was registered to the business. "Dammit."

I really didn't want to violate her privacy by emptying her purse. And I didn't have to. Just before I picked up her clutch, I looked up. Sinter stood before the hood, looking at me.

Fourteen

I rolled down my window. Sinter gave me an address on Washington Street.

"So," I said, "it would be a waste of time for me to ask how you know where she lives."

He answered with a flashing twinkle and said that he would meet us there.

I started the navigation system and selected a saved destination: home. The route lit up, and we were off, continuing down Whitehead Street. After several blocks of weaving my way through town, I pulled into the drive. The place had a tall security fence and a gate. I looked up and found two openers clipped to the visor. I picked one and got lucky.

As the gate opened, I saw Sinter, standing in the drive by the garage door. As I rolled closer, I pressed the second opener, the garage door lifted, and I drove inside.

I got Sylvia out of the car and carried her. I had her keys in my hand, and said, "Here, Sinter. Take these and unlock the door."

"That won't be necessary," he said, and opened the door.

I walked by, rolling my eyes, and he followed me in, flipping on lights. It was a large open floor plan, and we entered the kitchen. Across the room, by an enormous floor-to-ceiling window, sat a sofa. I took Sylvia there and laid her down gently. I sat on the edge and pushed her hair out of her eyes. From behind me I heard, "She'll be fine." After a few moments, I stood to face Sinter.

"Okay. Out with it. What's going on? What happened back there? And what does the dude dressed as a goat-man have to do with any of this?"

"His name is Krampus, and it's no costume."

"What are you talking about?"

"He is the Christmas Devil."

Oh, brother. Here we go again. "I've never heard of such."

"That would be because he usually stays around Germany and Austria. It was once thought we worked together. While I gave gifts to nice and pleasant children, he would scare naughty children into being nice. That, however, isn't the case. He is evil and spreads ill will among those that experience his presence. He's an extension of Satan and sucks the love out of people. Most people anyway. You have seen it for yourself."

"So, let me get this straight. This Krampus fella, who isn't just some guy in a fancy costume, is the Christmas Devil. He is real and the one responsible for all the hate and discontent back there?"

"Exactly. As well as the problems at the restaurant on Stock Island, the boat parade, and the brief commotion at the Green Parrot. When you did your push-ups."

That was right. I had seen him at the Green Parrot, but only for a few seconds. "But wait... how in the..."

This time, he rolled his eyes at me. "Stop denying it. You know deep down it all to be true."

"I know I feel like I'm losing my mind."

Sinter laughed. "No. You are perfectly sane and a good person."

"You see! Right there. I have you now. That's where you are wrong. I'm no angel, but I'm getting better."

"Nigel. Facing the truth is often never easy. And accepting the unimaginable can be harder. I know everything. I won't go into details. They're not pretty, but Virginia, Miami, even the boy and the snakes. I know all about them."

I turned around and walked over to look out the window. "Well, if you know about all that, I find it hard to believe you could consider me a good person."

"Let me put it this way, Nigel. The naughty list, as you like to call it, has a tendency to grow smaller where you're involved."

I turned back around. "This Krampus. He doesn't seem to affect me. Why is that?"

"Because you are a believer."

"You keep saying that. Why?"

"I need people like you to help me."

"Help you? Help you do what? You don't ride a sleigh, you don't go down chimneys, there are no elves in a workshop at the North Pole, and let's not forget the flying reindeer. They don't exist either. Do you even like milk and cookies, or is that a fabrication too?"

Sinter smiled. "I love milk and cookies."

"Okay. At least we have that. So, since the rest of the current Santa conventions aren't true, what do you do, and why do you need my help?"

"I am the opposite of Krampus, an extension of God. I spread the goodness of Christ during the season. Haven't you ever wondered how people become nicer and better examples of themselves during the season? How they become more charitable and giving? I help to bring that out in God's children. I don't deliver gifts anymore, but I help Jesus deliver His gift. The gift of hope and mercy."

I said nothing, but with a warmness in my heart thought, *You sound too good to be true.*

Sinter smiled. "Feels good, doesn't it?"

"What?"

"When the truth is too good to be true."

"You did it again! You read my mind!"

Sinter smiled again. "You are an open book. People that don't hide from their emotions usually are. Let me see... how did Mr. Gibson put it? Oh yes. 'Promise me you will never get so tough that you'll never have the need to cry. It will mean you have lost your soul. And always take care of and protect those that are defenseless.'"

I froze to a pounding beating in my heart. Not because of the flash that came from Sinter's eye. Not because he had recited words that had only been shared between myself and the late elementary school janitor that has become my mentor.

No. I froze at the voice. It had been decades since I heard it, but it was him, Mr. Gibson, speaking through Sinter.

"Yes, Nigel. It's all true, and he is quite proud of you and the person you have become."

I found a chair and sat, my hands held to my head in disbelief. But no, it wasn't disbelief; it was amazement and wonder.

Sinter and I shared a quiet moment as we looked at each other. Then a voice from the sofa got their attention. "Sinter? What are you doing here?"

Fifteen

I got up and went to Sylvia and sat on the edge of the sofa. I watched her gaze fall upon me. A smile stretched across her face.

Sinter said, "I'm going to leave you two for a bit. I'll be right outside."

After he left, I asked, "How do you feel? Are you okay?"

She nodded. "Okay, I guess. How did I get here?" She reached up and rubbed my arm. "Did I bring you home for a big night and pass out on you?"

"No. I brought you home. Don't you remember what happened?"

She turned her head, searching for her recent past. "Yes. It got crazy again. I was angry again... with some guy that..." She turned her head the other way.

"He tried to drag you away."

"It's all pretty foggy after that."

"Sylvia. How do you know Sinter?"

"Oh, he is the sweetest, silly man. He's been coming to SantaCon for years. He is fun and loving to be around. It feels good to be around him." She looked over my shoulder to make sure he hadn't come back in, and in a whisper said, "He thinks he's the real Santa, you know."

I looked back toward the door. "You're going to think I am crazy, but I'm pretty sure he is."

"What are you talking about?"

I did my best to recall and share with Sylvia everything I could remember about Kris Kringle, Saint Nicholas, Sinter, Santa Claus, and Krampus.

"I know I've screwed up trying to explain," I said, "but that pretty well sums it up."

"And you believe this stuff?"

"Call me crazy, but yeah, I think so."

"You're crazy."

At some point, Sinter had reentered the house. He startled us when he said, "He's not crazy. I threw a lot at you in a short amount of time, Nigel. I think you did a fine job."

I stood. "Sinter. What is Krampus doing here?"

"He is after me, to stop my work. He wants to stop the promise of Christmas."

"So what is it you need me to do?"

Sylvia sat up on the sofa. "Crazy talk. There is crazy talk going on in my house. Craziness I can't believe."

Sinter and I looked at her and in unison said, "You will."

Slowly Sinter made his way to her, took a seat, and asked, "Do you remember when you stopped believing in me, or in reality, the idea of me?"

"No."

"I do. You were seven years old. And despite your older brother's attempt to sabotage my existence, you continued to believe. But that year, when you tore the wrapping off a large present, it was a Kenner Easy Bake Oven." Sinter stopped and watched as Sylvia's memory came back and her eyelids opened wider. "But it wasn't the present that you saw. It was the Montgomery Ward price tag stuck on the front. Your father had forgotten to remove it before wrapping it. Your heart sank..."

"That's right," she said, "because I realized my brother had been right. Santa didn't bring presents. Mommies and daddies bought them." She looked at the floor, shaking her head.

"And you never played with that little oven, not once. It stayed in the corner of your room for two years until your dad took it to the Goodwill."

"That's right. How do you know all this?"

"It's okay, Sylvia," he said. "You can believe again. I still exist, just not as your innocent heart once thought."

Sylvia said nothing.

"Look at me," said Sinter.

She did, and the reflection of Sinter's twinkle flashed off her eyes.

I said, "There it is again."

She looked at me, and I nodded with a grin. "I know. It's crazy... but it's not." Then I looked at the old man. "So, Sinter. What do we do now?"

He turned to look at me. "We have to find him and stop him."

"Where is he?"

"I don't know. Out there somewhere."

"How do we stop him?"

"With goodness and the promise of Christmas."

"I don't understand."

"His impact," said Sinter, "is diminished by the pure spirit of Christmas. Remember, when you saw him at the Green Parrot, he had very little effect on people. That's because the place overflowed with the giving spirit. He hates that because it weakens him."

"Can't we just kill it?"

"No. I'm afraid not."

"But you said we need to stop him. How do we do that?"

"We have to catch him and lock him away in my church."

"Your church? Isn't that in Myra? As in Turkey?"

"Yes. That is correct."

Sylvia got up off the sofa and walked toward the kitchen. "I can't believe my ears. Y'all have gone cuckoo for Cocoa Puffs. May I get anyone a drink?"

"I'll take a water," said Sinter.

"Do you have Diet Coke?" I asked.

"No, I don't."

"Yes, you do," said Sinter.

Sylvia reached for the fridge door and opened it. "No, I really..." She stopped dead in her tracks, then looked at Sinter. "Where did these come from?"

He answered with a wink and a twinkle.

She grabbed herself a beer, Sinter a water, and my can of Diet Coke as she mumbled, "I'm losing my mind."

"Why Myra?" I asked.

"That is where my truest spirit and the power of Christmas lives. He is powerless there."

I took my Diet Coke from Sylvia. "Myra, Turkey. That's not exactly around the corner."

"No. It isn't, but we don't have to go to Turkey. I have many powerful churches throughout the world. All of them overflow with the goodness of the savior. Any of them will do."

"Do you have a church in Key West?"

"No. I'm afraid not."

Sylvia sat back down and jumped into the conversation. "So, exactly where is the closest Church of Saint Nick?"

With a smile, he said, "It's close, Sylvia; Christmas Key."

Sixteen

At 0407, my eyes opened up. Sylvia had her belly snuggled close to my side and an arm draped across my stomach. I was thankful for the invitation to stay the night. The thought of the trip back to the boat wasn't a pleasant one. I kissed her on the top of her head, and she sleepily kissed me back on my chest.

I let her sleep as I thought about the night before and right before Sinter left us to get some rest. He promised the next day would be a long one. Before he took off, I asked him where he was going.

"Christmas Key," he said.

"Where's that? How can we find you?"

"Don't worry. I'll find you. We have a week before the big holiday parade, so it's critical that we get Krampus before then. He preys on large gatherings, and one like that could be disastrous."

"Won't the parade be too festive for him to do any harm?" I asked.

"Festive, yes, but very secular and void of the true meaning of Christmas. Much like the SantaCon gathering. We have to grab him soon."

I slipped out from underneath Sylvia and made my way downstairs to the kitchen to find and start some coffee. As I poured water into the reservoir of the Keurig, I heard a groggy voice.

"I reached for you, and you weren't there. I thought you had gone."

She was standing at the bottom of the stairs, rubbing her eyes, and wearing my shirt that barely covered her butt.

"No. I've already told you once. I don't operate like that." I pointed at my shirt and said, "And besides, don't you think I'd probably want my clothes if I were going to leave?"

She looked down and pulled at my shirt to look at it. Then she looked up, smiling. "Oh, yeah. I guess so."

After dropping a pod in the machine and hitting the start button, I walked to her and pulled her body into mine for a hug. "I'm sorry to wake you. I was trying to be quiet."

"That's okay. I'm an early riser too. By the way, what time is it?"

"About three-thirty."

"Oh, crap. Not that early, though."

The Keurig machine gurgled and coughed the last of the brew in the cup. I turned my head to look, but she reached up and pulled my face back around.

"Forget the coffee. Come back to bed. Make love to me. After getting hot and sweaty, we can shower. Then I'll make us some breakfast."

"That's one hell of an offer."

"It's the best one you'll get all day."

I watched her turn around and slowly ascend the steps. She looked back at me over her shoulder and lifted my shirt enough to expose her butt cheeks. Then I started up the stairs. What's a man to do?

We made love again in her big shower, and it left us sitting on the long tile bench, panting. The hot, steamy water from the multiple showerheads bounced off our bodies as we caught our breath.

I said, "The shower idea was a good one."

Sylvia turned her head toward me and winked. "Wait until I serve up breakfast."

"Oh, brother. I don't think I can go another round."

"Me either, but it's a nice thought."

"Well, I guess it might depend on what you cook up. Do you have the makings for pancakes or French toast?"

"Yeah."

"With maple syrup?"

"Uh huh."

"I could think of some things to do with maple syrup."

We both had a long laugh. Then she grabbed a bar of soap and said, "I'll scrub your back, if you'll scrub mine."

She cooked naked under her towel wrapped hair. I sat at the table with a towel tied around my waist. We opted for eggs and bacon. I promised to make French toast another time. We were okay with that, as it gave us something to look forward to.

As she was turning the bacon, I said, "That place Sinter mentioned before he left, Christmas Key. Are you familiar with it?"

"No. There is Wisteria Island, also called Christmas Tree Island, but I don't know of an actual Christmas Key."

"It's just strange. He said that was where he was going last night. I guess he could just be making it up."

"Baby, there are a bunch of little islands out there."

"But would he do that?" I asked. "Make something up like that?"

Sylvia shrugged her shoulders. "Do you want toast with your eggs?"

"Yeah, that would be nice."

We ate our breakfast and said little between bites. I was thinking about Sinter and Krampus. I could tell she was too when she asked, "Do you really believe Sinter is the real Santa and this Krampus business?"

"No. Sinter is not Santa. At least not the rendition of Santa our parents taught us. He is Kris Kringle, though, Saint

Nicholas. That much I believe. And the Krampus business... I know it all sounds farfetched, but if I believe in Sinter, and I do, then I have to believe everything. Even Krampus."

She said nothing.

"And I saw the look in your eye when he mentioned the Easy Bake Oven. It had a convincing effect on you. Don't say it didn't." I chuckled and said, "Or he'll put you on the naughty list for lying."

"I have to admit. That was odd. I haven't thought about that morning in like forever."

"He knows things, Sylvia. Things nobody else would ever know. He's been throwing bits and pieces of my life in my face since I met him. He's special, and if you are going to be any help, you need to believe too."

She pushed her plate forward, scooted her chair back, and walked toward me. I pushed the table forward, and she stepped across my legs to straddle me. She gave me a gentle kiss and said, "It's all crazy, but I believe in you. That's for sure."

I watched her eyes as she came in for a longer kiss. When our lips parted, I said, "I know it isn't ideal, but I need to borrow your car."

"Take it," she said. "That means you'll be coming back."

"Yes, I'll be back. I won't be too long. Got to run by the boat and grab some fresh clothes. I didn't mean to rip my shirt in half when I tore it off you earlier."

She stuck her tongue out at me and held it there between her teeth. Then she raised her eyebrows and said, "Yes, *you* did, and *you* know it. Keys are in the bowl. Be careful, but hurry. I promise to be ready when you get back."

Seventeen

When I got to the marina, I had to park down by Navigator's. Which was probably a good thing. Steve saw the Jag and came outside. As he got closer, he didn't look right, and he walked with a limp. I rolled down the window. "What in creation happened to you? You look like a truck ran over you."

"Some sum bitch blindsided me last night. And for no reason, too. The whole place went to shit fast."

"Oh, that's right! You were there. Say no more. I was there for a while but got out of there when things got crazy. I heard it was bad."

"A damn riot is what it was. I tried to get out of there too, but the next thing I knew, I was out cold in the parking lot."

He leaned down to look in the window. "Where's Ms. Mason?"

"She's at home. I just came by for a change of clothes."

"Oh, I see."

"You see what?"

"I see you driving her car, and you didn't come home last night. I see you left her at *her* house, which means you were *there* this morning, which also suggests you stayed *there* last night. Now you are here to pick up clothes, which makes me think you will head back to her place. That is some friend you have there. Lucky you. Are you moving in or something?"

"You're a regular Lieutenant Columbo, Steve. And yes, we are just good friends, and no, I am not moving in. Now, will you just shut up and do me a favor?"

"What?"

"Help me get out of this damn thing!"

I changed into a pair of shorts, a Bowery Station t-shirt, and swapped my Sperry's for my running shoes. I was probably on the boat for less than seven minutes. In and out. I had places to be. I tried calling Sylvia to let her know I was on my way, but she didn't pick up.

Back on the road. It's a tight fit, but the Jag was fun to drive. The acceleration, speed, and handling were superb. Going through the base, you need to take it nice and slow, because the navy Po-po will pull you over for doing three over the limit. It seems to be like that on every naval base. But once I hit the loop that put me back on A1A, I opened it up and let the Jag do its thing. It was fun.

When I got on the island, I hung a left to stay on A1A to drive by the water. I slowed it down to enjoy the view. The sea and beaches were stunning. I eased around the bend where the highway becomes Bertha Street, then weaved through the residential streets until I approached Sylvia's street from Thompson Lane. As I pulled up to the stop sign and prepared to make a left, a black Suburban flew around the corner and almost hit me. "Son of a bitch, pal. Slow it down."

I stayed at the intersection for a few beats to catch my breath. Sylvia would have killed me if I scratched the Jag. As I made the turn onto Washington, I smiled. *No, she probably wouldn't have cared.*

A couple of houses before I got to Sylvia's, I reached up and hit the gate opener. But as I eased into the drive, the gate was closing. It had already been open. *Had I not closed it when I left?* As I watched the gate come together, I said, "Yes, you did." I hit the button again. As the gate opened back up, I noticed the garage door was open too. I pulled in nice and slow to take in my surroundings. Once in the garage, I saw the door to the kitchen was ajar. "I don't like the looks of this."

I got out of the car and headed toward the door. "Sylvia?"
No answer.
I nudged the door open with my knee. "Sylvia! I'm back!"
Nothing.
Entering the kitchen, I stopped in my tracks. There had been a struggle. Chairs from the dinette set lay overturned. A lamp lay broken on the floor. The coffee cup I had drunk from earlier lay smashed at the base of the wall. *Don't touch a thing, dammit.* I made my way up the steps to check upstairs. I called her name again and got nothing. The upstairs was empty. *Not*

good. As I made my way back down, I saw it. On the floor, next to the sofa, was Sinter's hat. I rushed to it and picked it up. *What in the hell happened here?* Then my thoughts returned to the SUV, and I dashed back out through the garage. As I rushed past the Jag, I came to a halt. Out in the middle of the road stood Krampus. He was looking at me, laughing.

"You son of a bitch! Where are they?"

He turned and ran down the street, still laughing. I followed and saw him turn the corner where the SUV almost took me out. But like before at SantaCon, when I made the turn in full stride, he was gone. The only difference was I could still hear the laughing. I stopped to listen, to help with a direction, but it was no good. The laughter seemed to come from everywhere. I turned and turned in the middle of the street. Then... it all went quiet. The only sound I could hear was the rapid beating of my heart.

Since the county stretches from way up in the Everglades down through to Key West, there are several Monroe County Sheriff's Offices scattered about. The one in Key West is by the golf course on Stock Island. The Jag came into the parking lot a little hot. I had to lock up the brakes, pulling into a spot, getting the attention of several deputies that were meandering about. I ignored them as I unfolded myself from the car and dashed inside.

I went to the first person I saw, a female deputy attending a reception desk. "I need to report a kidnapping."

"Excuse me?"

"A double kidnapping, actually."

"Slow down and start by giving me your name."

I pulled out my wallet and withdrew my driver's license. "Here. My name is Nigel Logan. And I believe two people have been abducted."

She handed my license back. "You believe? Did you see it happen?"

"Well, no. But..." I stopped myself from going any further. It occurred to me I had to be careful with just how much I could share. If I went on about Sinter and Krampus, they would likely chalk me up as another Key West loony bird and throw my butt into a rubber room.

"Sir? You were saying."

"One of the people; it's Sylvia Mason."

"Ms. Mason, you say?"

"That is correct. I drove her car here."

"And who might the other person be?"

"I'm not totally sure," I lied.

"But you say Ms. Mason is involved? When did all this happen?"

"Just recently. It was a black Suburban... I think."

She looked at me with suspicious eyes and asked me to take a seat while she made a call. A few minutes later, she came from around her desk, holding out a phone. "Here," she said, "it's for you."

"Hello."

It was Sheriff Reynolds. He asked me what this was all about and how Ms. Mason was involved. I told him as much as I could without sounding like a fruitcake, and he agreed to meet me at her place to review the scene.

When I pulled into the drive, the sheriff's car was already there. He stood, leaning up against his hood. I could tell he was sizing me up as I approached. We shook hands. "Thank you for coming."

He looked back toward the house. "Okay. Walk me through it."

Again, I told him everything I could, minus the obvious as I took him through the house.

"Well," he said, "something went on here, but there is no sign of forced entry. Have you touched anything?"

"No, sir. Not since I came back this morning."

"But you were here?"

"Yes, sir. I told you that. She let me borrow her car, and when I came back, this is what I found."

"Well. It isn't much. Turned-over chairs, a broken lamp, and a smashed coffee cup don't necessarily add up to a crime scene. Hell, she could have had a fit and done all this herself."

We walked back out to the cars. "So, what are you going to do?"

"There isn't much I can do. It's been what, maybe an hour since you found the place like this. She could be anywhere. But, since it's Ms. Mason, I will put the word out for my deputies to keep an eye out for her."

"We got to do something. Time is ticking."

"Until we have something, we can't do anything. If you can produce evidence of an actual crime, I'll be happy to get more involved. Until then, I won't waste the time of my detectives and staff, period."

I said nothing.

"Listen, if you want to waste your money and somebody else's time, call Cam Derringer."

"Cam Derringer?"

I gazed at the ground searching for a memory. *Why does that name sound familiar?*

"Yeah, he's a private investigator and often a pain in my ass." He took out a pen and a notepad and jotted something down. Then he ripped off the page and handed it to me. "Here's his number and address. He's a live-aboard boat bum."

I took the paper and looked at the marina address, and my foggy memory began to clear with little details from a time long ago. *Could it be the same guy? How can it not be? How many Cam Derringers can there be... in Key West or anywhere else for that matter?* I looked up at the sheriff with a feigned smile. "Sounds like my kind of guy," I lied again.

As I drove to the marina, our past connection became clearer.

It was a long time ago, before Port St. Joe and any reason to leave Norfolk, Virginia. I was still aboard the USS Davenport. She and ship's company had been assigned a three-month deployment into the northern Caribbean Basin to work alongside the Coast Guard and the DEA on drug interdiction operations. It was mid-summer and hot as hell, but I'd been on worse missions. We stayed at sea for a week or two, intervening and inspecting suspicious craft, then we would pull into USCG Base, Sector Key West for a few days for liberty.

On one of the earlier liberty calls, some of the chiefs from the base invited me out for a night on the town. One of the guys, I can't remember his name, knew a fella that was having a dock party down at one of the marinas. It was promised that there would be no shortage of beautiful women or booze. That being a favorite combination, I agreed to tag along.

Long story short, the place was buzzing with activity: music, drinks, and oh yeah... women. Beautiful women. The odds of finding suitable female companionship were encouraging. The ratio of gals to guys had to be around five to three, and I was in the mood.

I wasn't sure of the occasion, but it was a great party. We hadn't been on the dock two minutes before we were led to the drink well and told to help ourselves. I hadn't met our host yet, but I couldn't wait to introduce myself.

While meandering the docks and working on my third Jim Beam, my eyes found a gorgeous blond whose eyes had already found me. She was leaning against a railing. I stopped in my tracks, and she added a smile. She was tall and fit, muscular legs and arms. Not overdone, but firm and sculpted. Her deep, bronze skin looked great as it showcased her short, black evening dress.

I moved toward her, and she stood from the rail to greet me. Yes, she was tall, maybe six-one. I wasn't sure what she was thinking at the time, but the only thing that came to my mind was, *Just my size.*

Dammit! What was her name? It doesn't matter. That night she was going to be mine. We had drinks and danced to perpetual Jimmy Buffett tunes. Then she kissed me and asked if I could walk her home. I kissed her back. A fire was being kindled.

The next thing I knew, somebody grabbed me by the shoulder and swung me around. I tripped and fell to my knees. My attacker looked down at me and said, "What do you think you are doing?"

I stood prepared to launch a full offensive, but a couple of the chiefs grabbed me.

"I could ask the same of you, pal."

"She's with me," he said.

"No, she isn't. I saw her first."

"I brought her here. She's my... was my date."

I looked at the blond and said, "He's kidding, right?"

She looked back, shrugged her shoulders, and bit her bottom lip.

"Really?" I said. "Aren't you a piece of work."

The guy said, "You can have her. Take her and leave."

I shook off the other chiefs and turned to leave. The blond started with me. I stopped. "Where do you think you're going?"

And that is how I first came to meet Cam Derringer.

Over the next couple months, we would often run across each other while in town. There would always be an acknowledgement of the other, but it was always cold and distant. We never spoke. What was there to talk about?

That was about to change.

From outside the marina gate, I sat in the car wondering if he would remember me. It was such a long time ago. How could he? After rehearsing my pitch for the hundredth time, I couldn't help but struggle with the idea of mentioning Sinter and Krampus. *Get a move on, Logan. The clock is ticking.* I climbed out of the car and headed to the gate. I stopped to look at the dock, it was as I remembered it. I pushed the gate, and the hinges screeched, begging for oil. The first boat I came to was a houseboat. Two beautiful gals sat in the shade of the forward deck.

"Hey, mister," one of them said in a friendly voice. "What cha looking for?"

I smiled. It was something I was used to; dockmates, keeping an eye out for each other. I was a stranger. I didn't belong. They had every right to be nosey.

"My name is Nigel Logan. Maybe you can help me. I am looking for" I took the paper out of my pocket and pretended to give it another glance. "...a Cam Derringer."

"Well, hello, Nigel. I'm Stacy, and this is Barbie. Pleased to meet you."

"Is Cam in trouble?" Barbie asked.

Stacy added, "Again?"

They both laughed.

"No, but somebody else might be. I'm hoping he might help."

Having passed some sort of test, the two girls nodded at each other in agreement.

"That's him right over there," said Stacy, pointing, "on the back deck of that boat."

I pretended to tip my hat and said, "Thank you very much."

Eighteen

Part II: Cam Derringer

"Cam!" Diane called. "Do you want a roll?"

"Sure," I said.

I was standing on the rear deck of my boat when my phone rang. It was my insurance company. My boat had sustained some damage from a storm that came through last week. "Yeah, this is Cam Derringer," I said.

The adjuster wanted me to briefly describe the damage to my boat. As I was doing so, I watched a man out of the corner of my eye. He was walking our way. When I glanced at him, I recognized the tall, muscular figure. He wasn't a friend, and he certainly hadn't been invited, so why would he be approaching my boat?

I haven't seen or talked to this fella in several years, since we got into an argument over a woman. He tried to steal her from me. I couldn't remember who the girl was or what she looked like, but it didn't matter. It was a short relationship that ended that night. I wasn't sure how long he'd been in town, but I'd seen him around. Mostly at Sloppy Joe's, starting about four months ago. We didn't speak. There was no reason.

As he strolled down the dock, I caught his stare and friendly smile. Diane came out carrying a tray of honeybuns and joined me. He stopped short of the stern. "Cam Derringer?" he asked.

Diane and I looked at each other, and she said, "Maybe."

He seemed to ignore the little game. "Mr. Derringer, my name is..."

"Logan," I interrupted, "Nigel Logan. I remember who you are."

The man named Logan said, "I remember you, too. Are you still holding a grudge?"

"Cam? Do you know this guy?" Diane asked.

"Yeah. From a long time ago. I'll tell you about it sometime. Logan, this is my daughter, Diane."

"You're on first-name basis with your daughter?"

"Not biological, and she's not available. So, keep your damn hands to yourself."

"Pay him no mind, Mr. Logan," said Diane. "He's always over-protective that way."

"Please, both of you, call me Nigel, and it's nice to meet you."

"So, Nigel" I said, "to what do I owe the pleasure of your being here?"

"Well, you're not going to believe it, but I need your help."

"What kind of help, Logan?"

"Missing persons. I need you to help me to find somebody, two somebodies, actually."

I looked Logan over for a while. He seemed sincere and truthful. The look on his face was full of concern and worry. "Hump," I grunted. A lot of water has passed under this hull over the years.

"Will you help me?"

"Come on board," I sighed. "We were about to have a Wild Turkey and a chocolate honeybun."

He climbed aboard. "I've been on a bit of a diet and don't drink that much anymore, but given the circumstances, I could use a stiff drink."

"Then pull up a chair."

He did and sat while Diane fetched him a glass of ice. She came back and gave him a nice long pour. He picked up a honeybun and took a bite.

I said, "Pretty damn tasty, huh?"

Nigel nodded. "What happened to that nice little houseboat you used to live on?" he asked as he looked around at my fifty-five-foot Kattie's deck.

"It blew up a few years ago."

"Too bad. I hope it wasn't serious."

"Terrorists."

"Interesting. I'd love to hear about it. I hate those bastards."

"Another time, maybe. So, what do you need?"

Nigel chewed and held up a finger. *Wait a sec.* He swallowed and said, "First, I need to ask you a question."

"Ask away."

"Do you believe in Santa Claus?" Then, while watching me over the rim of his glass, he took a long sip of his bourbon.

"Santa Claus?" I asked.

"That's right, Santa Claus," Nigel repeated. "But he prefers to be called Sinter."

I looked him in the eye, trying to see if he was serious. He appeared to be and stared back at me with a determined look. I guessed he was.

"Yeah," I said slowly. "I believe in Santa Claus."

He nodded and smiled slightly, as if this answered some question he had been unsure of.

"Good," he said, leaning back in his chair. "Because I need your help finding him, and to..."

"And, what?"

"And to save Christmas."

I almost choked on my bourbon. "Is that why you came here? You want me to find Santa and save Christmas?"

"Sinter, and yeah."

He nodded again and unfolded a piece of paper that had been tucked away inside his pocket.

"Do you know these people?" he asked, handing the paper to me.

On it were two names: Kris Kringle and Sylvia Mason. My eyes widened as I read the names again, not quite believing what I was seeing. *How could there be any connection between these two?*

I said, "I do know of a guy around here who claims his name is Kris Kringle. If it's the same person, I think he's a whack job but a very nice man. As for Sylvia, yeah, we know her."

"Good."

"Maybe Diane could help *you* more than me. She's a psychiatrist."

Nigel said, "I'm not a psycho."

I looked over at Diane, who had been quietly sipping her drink and observing the conversation. She set her glass down and turned to face us.

"I'm happy to help in any way I can," she said, her voice calm and professional. "But I have to admit, I'm a bit confused. What does Santa Claus have to do with anything?"

Nigel leaned forward; his eyes intense. "Sinter," he corrected. "It's a long story, but I'll give you the short version."

He told us everything he had been through. I kept glancing toward Diane. *Is this guy crazy? Do we need to make him a reservation for a rubber room?*

When he finished, I looked at Diane, who shrugged and took a sip of her drink. "I don't know anything about finding Sinter," she said with a small laugh. "But I can try to help with Sylvia. We're friends."

Nigel looked relieved. "That would be great."

"Nigel, have you been listening to yourself? It all sounds very..."

Nigel shook his head. "Crazy. I know, but I need your help, Cam. I need you to help me find Sinter and Sylvia. It's very important."

I knew that if Nigel was asking for my help, it must be for a good reason. Our history isn't that of two close friends.

"Are you talking about one of the Santas from the festival?"

"No, Cam. I'll say it again. I'm talking about the real Sinter. Kris Kringle."

"Alright," I said finally, taking another sip of bourbon. "Tell me *everything* you know."

Nigel repeated how he ran into Sinter at the Conch Republic Seafood bar. He had become convinced that this guy was the real deal.

He explained about Krampus and Sylvia and how it all led him here. As kooky as it all sounded, he was convincing and didn't appear to be lying.

"You've definitely piqued my curiosity, Nigel," I told him. "I'll go with you into town, and we'll take a look around. See what we can find. This Krampus fella seems to have taken a shine to you. If it's all on the up and up, then he's trying to get to you for some reason."

"That's all I ask for, Cam. I need some help. It'll take more than one person to find them."

"I'm busy this afternoon," Diane said, "but I can help later today."

"Okay, call me when you're free, and we'll get together."

Nigel and I stood and bid farewell to Diane. We headed to town to find the real Santa Claus. That's something I never thought I'd be doing.

We started at the Conch where he first saw him. It was packed with Santas. All of them were rather drunk.

"Do you see anyone who looks like this guy Kris?" I asked Nigel.

He looked around and told me Kris doesn't look like a typical Santa. "Sinter says these guys are way off. They're dressed like this because of the description in, 'Twas the Night Before Christmas."

"Really? That shatters my memories of Christmas. But it does align with the guy I was talking about."

"After you meet this guy, you'll have new memories of Christmas, and you'll love them."

"Let's check the street," I said.

We walked to the door and stepped onto the street. It was teeming with people, most of them in Christmas costumes.

Suddenly, there was a commotion in the middle of the street. A fight had broken out between around twenty people. They were throwing punches, and it looked like it would not end anytime soon.

"Krampus!" Nigel cried out in shock. "He's around here somewhere! We have to stop this!"

We stepped into the street and started trying to pull people off each other. There were too many. We needed help. I turned to find more volunteers to help, but now everyone on the sidewalk was fighting too.

Suddenly we heard loud laughter. It was a haunting sound from the other side of the street.

Nigel pointed at a creature that looked half goat and half human. I would have thought it was a costume, but Nigel yelled, "Krampus!"

We ran toward him. When he saw us coming, he turned and charged in the opposite direction. We chased him through the crowded street, dodging Santas and elves as we went.

Krampus was fast, but we were gaining on him. Suddenly, he darted down an alleyway. We followed him, but as we turned the corner, we were met with a dead end.

"Where did he go?" Nigel asked, panting heavily.

I scanned the area but found no sign of the creature. Then a door appeared at the end of the alley.

"He must have gone through there," I said, pointing to the small, unmarked door at the end of the alleyway.

We cautiously made our way to the door, which was slightly ajar. Nigel pushed it open, and we stepped inside.

The room was dimly lit, and the air was thick with the smell of incense. In the center of the room stood a woman dressed in a flowing white robe. She had long, dark hair and piercing blue eyes that seemed to look right through us.

"Who are you?" she asked, her voice soft but commanding.

"We're looking for Krampus," Nigel said, somewhat out of breath.

The woman's eyes narrowed. "And what makes you think you'll find him here?"

Nigel hesitated for a moment before explaining about his encounter with Santa and Krampus and how they were led to this location. "Krampus just ran in here," he said.

The woman listened intently, then nodded. "I see," she said, walking over to a table on the far side of the room. "I may be able to help you."

She picked up a small, ornate box and opened it. Inside was a single piece of paper. She handed it to me. I read it out loud.

"Ha, ha! You can't catch me!"

We looked back at the woman. Right before our eyes, she turned into Krampus, laughed, and disappeared in a puff of smoke.

I looked at Nigel. His eyes looked like two saucers. "I told you," he said, without looking away from where Krampus had been.

"Yes, you did. To tell you the truth, I only came along to humor you, but..."

We turned to leave, but there was no door behind us.

"What the hell?" I said.

"How're we going to get out of here?" Nigel asked.

We walked around the room, pressing on the cold stone walls. There didn't seem to be any way to escape the dungeon-like room.

"Maybe there's an opening in the ceiling," Nigel said.

We both looked up. "I don't see anything," I said. "I'll get on the table and take a look."

I pushed myself up on the table. When I did, a puff of smoke came up from the floor, and a trap door opened below the table.

"That's where he went," Nigel said. "It was a trick, not magic."

"Yeah, but that doesn't explain the door being gone or the woman that was here first."

"No, nothing will explain that. Shall we drop down and see what's there?"

"After you."

Nigel dropped through the trap door, then I followed. There was a room below about the size of the one above. We saw a door on one wall. It was wide open, inviting us to enter. This was really strange because, except for the Hemingway House, I don't know of any other basements in Key West.

We passed through the door into another world. Well, it might not have been another world, but it sure as hell wasn't Key West.

I turned around to make sure the door didn't close on us. It was gone.

Nineteen

"Where are we?" I asked.

"I don't know, but we're not in Kansas anymore."

The countryside we were in looked as if it could be a part of our earth, but it wasn't anywhere in the Keys or the United States. I was sure of that.

"Nigel, what the hell did you get me into?"

We were standing next to a dirt road. Where it led to was anyone's guess.

"Which way do you want to go?" Nigel asked.

"Well, we're facing that way," I said, pointing ahead of us, "let's go in that direction."

We walked for fifteen minutes, then heard something behind us. We turned around and stopped in the middle of the road.

A man and woman in a donkey cart full of straw rolled up to us and stopped.

"Hello," I said.

"Hello," the man said in a heavy German accent.

"Can you tell me where we are?"

They looked at each other and smiled.

"Dorsten," she said, then winked at me, "Krampus?"

Nigel and I looked at each other astonished.

"Yes," I said, then asked, "Germany?"

She nodded. "You are the chosen ones this year."

"The chosen ones?"

"Get in the back of the wagon, and we'll explain on the way."

We jumped on the side of the flat cart and stared at the two in anticipation.

"First of all," the woman said as the man guided the cart down the road, "the two of you should feel honored."

"Honored for what?" I asked.

Every year Krampus selects two people and brings them here for his celebration."

"What celebration?"

"Today is December 5th. It's Krampus Day, the day before St. Nicholas Day."

"Krampus Day? Never heard of it, and why do the two of you speak such good English?"

"When you are talking, I hear the German language. When I am talking, you hear English. That's just the way it works today."

I looked around at the wagon and the countryside and asked, "What year is this?"

"1488," the woman said.

I looked at Nigel. "Nigel, I swear if we get out of this alive, I'll..."

"Now calm down, Cam," the woman said. "You wouldn't be here if Krampus didn't want you here. He made sure the two of you would arrive together."

"Are we going to get to go back home?" Nigel asked.

"If you're good," she said and laughed.

We were quiet as the cart rolled on toward Dorsten.

As we approached the town, I couldn't help but feel uneasy. The people we passed on the road looked at us with a mix of fear and reverence. It was as if they knew something we didn't. The woman guiding the cart noticed my unease and placed a hand on my shoulder.

"Krampus is not to be feared," she said. "He is simply the punisher of the naughty children. He rewards the good ones."

I nodded, still unsure of what was happening. As we entered the town, I noticed that the buildings were old and made of stone. The people dressed in medieval clothing and spoke in old German. It was as if these people loved Krampus.

The cart eventually came to a halt in front of a large wooden building. The woman led us inside and into a room filled with people dressed in elaborate costumes. A figure wearing a terrifying mask and a fur coat stood at the front of the room, holding a whip in one hand and a sack in the other.

"Welcome, chosen ones," the figure said in a deep, booming voice. "You have been brought here to witness the punishment of the naughty children."

Krampus's face filled our vision. His long teeth, sharp as knives, were centimeters away. He bared them, ready to rip open our throats.

I exchanged a nervous glance with Nigel. We had to play along if we wanted to find a way out of this. The figure known as Krampus gestured for us to follow him as he stepped inside another room.

The door slammed behind us. He turned toward us with an evil grin. He raised a large sword over his head and said, "I have brought you here to die because you are not believers. No punishment will come to me." Then he brought the sword down, swinging it toward us.

"Cam!" I heard my name. "Cam!" Then I felt a hand on my shoulder. "Cam!"

I turned around.

"Are you okay?" Diane asked. "What are you two doing standing in this alley?"

"What?"

"I just saw the two of you run into the alley. What are you doing?"

I turned and looked at Nigel. The puzzled look on his face told me I was not the only one who didn't understand what had just happened to us. I looked back at Diane. "Krampus," I said. "We were chasing him. He ran in here."

"I didn't see y'all chasing anyone," she said. "I just saw the two of you running down the street, then turning down this dead-end alley. That was just about thirty seconds ago. I thought I'd better come and find out what the problem was."

Nigel said, "This is just too weird, man."

"You think Krampus wasn't even here? Can he make us see things like that?"

"Beats me," said Nigel. "I don't know. All I know is, I haven't seen anything like this before."

"What did you experience in the last few minutes?" I asked him.

"We were in Germany, 1488, riding on a cart going to Dorsten. Krampus was there and about to cut us in half with a sword. Then we were back here again."

"Yeah, that's the same thing. I saw. But... the woman told us it was December the 5th. Today is the seventeenth. SantaCon."

We stepped out of the alley and looked down the street. No one was fighting. Everyone was still partying. Christmas music filled the air.

"We've got our work cut out for us," I said.

Diane said, "Maybe I should make an appointment for the two of you to come to my office and lie down on my couch for a while."

"Diane," Nigel said, "I swear we saw Krampus run into the alley, and then somehow, we were transported to Germany. If you hadn't called to us, we might have been sliced and diced."

"Well, you're here now, and I don't think we're any closer to finding Sinter or Sylvia."

I looked at Nigel. "Where do we go from here?"

"Do you believe me now?"

"I believe we may have been drugged. We're seeing things that can't be true, but I'm in it with you. I'll help you find out what's going on."

Then Diane reached up and pulled a piece of straw from Nigel's shirt. "What's this?"

Nigel and I looked at the straw and then at each other.

"Let's go," Nigel said.

The three of us walked down the street silently, lost in our thoughts, but understanding we were up against something a lot bigger than us.

"Nigel," Diane asked, "when was the last time you saw Sylvia?"

"At her house this morning. She let me use her car to run an errand, and when I returned, the house looked like a crime scene. She was gone, and Sinter was gone. I saw a black SUV leaving and then Krampus at the end of the driveway."

"Can he drive a car?" I asked.

"That I don't know," Nigel replied. "But he was definitely there. And now we've seen him in person, in two different eras. There's no denying his existence."

We turned down a side street, and I noticed a man walking towards us. He was tall and muscular, with short blond hair and sparkling blue eyes. He looked like he could be a model, but there was something dangerous about him.

I felt Diane's hand slip into mine, and I turned to see her looking at me with concern. She knew when danger was near.

"Hello, Cam," the man said, stopping in front of us. "Hello, Nigel."

I looked at Nigel. The look on his face told me that he didn't know the man either.

"Do you know him?" I asked Nigel.

He shook his head. "No, I don't."

The man smiled and said, "I'm here to help you capture Krampus."

We all looked at him in disbelief. How could he possibly know what we were trying to do?

The man continued, "I'm a hunter of sorts. I've been tracking Krampus for some time now and have come up with a plan that will help us catch the beast. We need to set up a trap using various items such as garlic, holy water, silver bullets, and other mystical objects that can act as wards against evil spirits and monsters like Krampus."

He went on to explain how he had tracked Krampus from Europe to America and was certain he knew where the creature was hiding. He then offered his services as an experienced tracker and hunter in exchange for our promise to let him have Krampus.

"What makes you think we're looking for Krampus?" Nigel asked.

"I saw you with him in Germany. 1488. I was there."

"How'd you get back here?" I asked.

"There's a portal. I'll show you where it is once we capture him. It will give you the ability to time travel. Are you interested?"

"Give us a minute," I said and stepped away from the man with Nigel and Diane.

"What do ya think?" I asked them.

Diane said, "It's worth a try. We don't have anything else to go on."

"Sinter mentioned something about another island, Christmas Key," Nigel said. "But I've never heard of it. He might have taken them there."

"Yeah," I said. "That's not much to go on. I know all the Keys around here, and I've never heard of Christmas Key."

"I say we give this guy a chance," Nigel said. "He's a total whack job just like me and you. After all, he was in Germany with us."

We agreed that we would give him the rest of the day to prove himself and then if we hadn't gotten any closer, we'd cut ties with him.

After telling him our conditions, he gave us his address and told us to be there in an hour. Then, *Poof!* He disappeared.

"Shit," said Nigel. "I wish folks would quit doing that."

"Come on," I said. "Let's grab a bite to eat and then head to Sugarloaf Key. I've never heard of this street."

We grabbed a burger at Wendy's and headed north on U.S. One.

When we arrived at Sugarloaf a half-hour later, we found ourselves standing in front of an old Victorian-style house surrounded by a tall fence topped with barbed wire.

I've never seen this place before," I said.

"Me either," Diane said. "Where'd it come from?"

We entered through an ivy-covered gate and followed a winding path until we reached the door. The hunter was there waiting for us, looking older than he had only an hour ago but still fit enough to tackle whatever lay ahead of us on this quest.

He welcomed us warmly inside and showed us around his home, which was filled with all sorts of curiosities from across the globe—weapons and artifacts from long-ago battles against monsters like Krampus were neatly arranged along the walls. Ancient books lined the shelves, which reached almost all the way up to the high ceiling in places.

There were no sounds coming from within the house, only the distant rumble of cars driving by on the road outside, and a faint echo of birds singing in the trees.

The house was filled with the musty smell of aged books and mildew, along with faint wafts of incense and smoke from candles burning in the corners.

He explained that each object held a special memory. "Once I capture Krampus, my mission will be complete. At one time, he was a good person who only punished bad children. He wouldn't harm them, but he would scare them with his switches. Some kids would even think he would eat them or drag them to Hell. Now, though, he has started to cause trouble between adults. You saw the fights. He's turning evil. He wants to stop Christmas. With your help, I think we can stop him."

Nigel nodded in agreement. "Exactly! We need to capture him and lock him in Sinter's dungeon."

"Nigel," I said. "I want it to go on record here. I will help you because something is wrong, but there is no such thing as Santa or Sinter."

"You gotta believe, Cam," said Nigel. "Besides, if you don't believe in Sinter, how do you explain Krampus?"

"Nigel, listen to yourself. First of all, you think you've been sleeping with one of the hottest girls in Key West. That's far-fetched enough, but now you want me to believe that Krampus has kidnapped Santa and Sylvia. I think you're on some kind of a drug."

"Sinter, not Santa, and I don't do drugs."

"Nigel is right, Cam. Sinter is real," the hunter said.

"What are you talking about? You're not even real," I said. "What's your name?"

"I am Dietmar Voigt, the hunter of evil. I work for the goodness in the world."

"The goodness. Where do you find that?"

"It's all around us. Most people are afraid to let it out. They keep it inside and only show their meanness on the outside. I'm surprised that Diane doesn't believe in Sinter. She's a good person."

Diane took a step toward Dietmar. "Cam is one of the best people I know. He would never harm anyone who didn't deserve it."

Dietmar smiled. "There you go, Cam. You have a believer. She believes in you."

"And I believe in her, but I just don't believe in Santa Claus."

"Sinter," Nigel exclaimed.

I shook my head. "Okay, what do we do now?"

Dietmar clapped his hands together. "We make a plan to find Krampus! We must first figure out where he is hiding. I believe that the best way to do this is to follow the clues he has left behind." He pointed to the shelves of ancient books, many of which were written in different languages. "These books may contain clues about Krampus's whereabouts. We can use them to track him down."

He then pulled out a large map and spread it across the table. It was an old map with strange symbols and markings, but Dietmar seemed to understand what they meant. "This map shows us all the places where Krampus has been known to hide over the years," he said. He pointed at various spots on the map as he spoke. "He often hides in caves or secluded forests, so these are likely areas we should search first."

Nigel nodded in agreement, grabbed a book, and said, "Well, you ain't gonna find any caves around here." He thumbed through the pages. "I don't even know what in the hell to look for."

In the meantime, Diane and I started looking around for anything else that might help us. After a few minutes of searching, Dietmar said we had gathered enough information to start piecing together a plan of action: we would travel from place to place following any leads we could find until, eventually, we found our prey.

We decided that Dietmar would take point on this mission due to his knowledge of hunting and tracking, while Diane, Nigel, and I followed up with research into any other potential leads or clues that might be useful during our quest. With a plan in place, all four of us set off on our journey, determined to capture Krampus before Christmas.

Twenty

"Where do we start?" I asked Dietmar.

"We don't have far to go. Krampus loves the Keys because he can cause havoc so easily here. The drunken sailors hanging out in the bars love to fight. One, in particular, is the Hook Line Bar in Upper Sugarloaf. We'll start there."

"Yeah, I know it. It's close," I said. "But it's kind of a dangerous place. Walter and I got in a fight the last time we were there."

"Walter?" Dietmar asked.

"My golden retriever."

"You're a dog lover."

"Only Walter."

"What about Hank?"

"Yeah, I love Hank too. How do you know Stacy's dog?" I asked curiously.

"I guess I should tell you. I checked you out before I chose you. I already had my eye on Nigel. He led me to you and Diane."

This guy was giving me the creeps. He knows too much about me. He lives in a house that I could swear wasn't there two weeks ago, and he believes that Santa is a real person.

"Shall we," I said, and led them to my Land Rover.

On the way to the bar, I told them I didn't think anyone would be there. "They're all going to be partying at SantaCon in Key West."

"We'll see," Dietmar said.

When we pulled into the parking lot, I had to hunt for a space to park.

Nigel said, "Place looks crowded to me."

I saw Tony Wilks walking in the front door. He was wearing a Santa hat.

"I've never seen him wearing anything like that," I said.

"No, me either," Diane said. "The last time we were here, he was beating on Glen Clem."

Then we both noticed, at the same time, that Glen was getting out of his car and heading for the door. "Oh shit," I said. "This isn't going to be good. We better get in there."

"Let's go," Dietmar said excitedly, opening his door.

We raced toward the entrance, the door swinging open with a rush of Christmas music. My eyes widened when I saw Glen and Tony laughing together, wearing matching red and white Santa hats. Everywhere we looked, people had donned festive holiday apparel, from green velvet Mrs. Claus dresses to candy cane-striped scarves. A banner hung across one wall reading *"Welcome To The Real SantaCon."*

"I think this was an epic waste of time," Dietmar said. "Let's go."

"Hold up," I said. "I want to spend some time with these guys. Let's catch up."

Nigel said, "Let's go, Cam. We don't have time for this."

"Sure, we do. Come on."

I grabbed Nigel by the arm and led him through the throng of merrymakers. They all welcomed him warmly, offering drinks as soon as I introduced him as my friend. Glancing back at Dietmar and Diane, I noticed Diane surrounded by five men gyrating to the beat of the music, her hair spinning around her head as she held a beer bottle in one hand and waved it in the air like a staff of authority. The poor sap who tried to mess with her would surely get more than he bargained for—she could take any man down in seconds flat.

A few minutes later, I felt someone grab my arm. It was Dietmar. "Come on, Cam. We must go now. We have work to do."

I knew he was right. I bid farewell to my friends. Nigel found Diane and led her out to the parking lot.

Once we were all together again, I asked Dietmar, "Where are we going now?"

"Ramrod Key," he said.

We drove south, through the night, passing through the other Keys along the way. Every few miles, Dietmar would stop and get out of the car for a few minutes. I had no idea what he was doing, but it seemed important to him, so I didn't ask questions. As we waited in the car, he walked back and forth in front of the headlights, talking to himself. Very strange.

The third time he did this, Nigel said, "And you think I'm a looney bird."

I didn't reply.

Finally, we arrived at Ramrod Key. The air was full of stars, and the moon shone brightly over the trees. The water lapped gently against the shore, and we all felt an incredible peace wash over us as soon as we stepped out of the car.

"What are we doing here?" I asked.

"Listen," Nigel said. "Do you hear it?"

I listened, trying hard to pick up what he was talking about. Finally, I heard it. There was singing. It sounded like it was coming from the beach. We were at the Ramrod Swimming Hole. It's a secluded public beach.

The music became louder as we walked toward the beach. Then with the help of the moonlight, we could see a bonfire. Around it was a host of people singing Christmas carols. We moved into the light of the fire.

"Cam!" I heard someone yell. "Come on in."

I shielded my eyes so I could see. It was Dave from Key West. He's a bartender at Schooners and a good friend. Sitting next to him was Crazy Wanda, his girlfriend.

"What are you doing here?" I asked.

"We came to celebrate Christmas with my family."

I never thought of Dave as having a family.

We stepped closer into the circle. The guitar player stopped and told us to get a beer out of the cooler.

"Diane! It's me, Ryan" It was Ryan Chase, a local sheriff deputy in Key West. He has been dating Stacy on and off for a few years. "Have a seat."

I was surprised to see these people here. I thought they would be in Key West for SantaCon. Dave was always up for a huge party. Ryan, I thought, would be on duty at the festival.

I introduced Nigel as my friend again. We spent an hour laughing and singing. Diane danced with most of the guys there. Just when I had forgotten our troubles, Dietmar said. "Cam, it's time. Krampus isn't around here. These people are true believers. We must go search for him. It's going to be too late if we don't move quickly."

Diane came to my side and took my hand. "What's going on?"

"I don't know. I didn't know Dave had family here."

"Me either."

We looked at each other for a bit, then turned and walked to the car.

When we were in the car, a thought came to me. "Dietmar, do you think maybe Krampus left those clues to lead us here? Do you think he is biding time to get Sinter and Sylvia away from us?"

"That is a good point, Cam. You know these Keys better than anyone. Where is the most dangerous place to be at night in all the Keys? That might be where we find him."

I thought for a minute. "To be honest, it's Key West. I think he's been leading us away from there, and we have fallen for his scheme."

"Hurry then. We must get back to Key West. We'll be able to find him, if he's there. There will be trouble around him."

We drove back to Key West in tense silence. As we drove toward the docks, I could see the lights of SantaCon still going strong. We had a long way to go before we found Krampus, but at least now we knew where he was headed.

We all felt tense and nervous. As we drove down Duval Street, we saw Krampus walking with a group of people, laughing and talking. He had a large bag over his shoulder, and he was wearing a black coat and hat.

Then we saw another Krampus across the street. Then another in the next block.

"Costumes," Diane said. "We'll never find the real one."

"Let me out here," Dietmar said. "I'll search on foot."

I stopped the car, and he got out. "I'll find you," he said and disappeared into the crowd.

We kept searching for the real Krampus. There were too many fakes in costumes. It was getting confusing.

But then, just as I was about to give up hope, we heard someone shouting down an alleyway.

Diane hopped out of the car to follow the noise, but Nigel stopped her. "Let me go after him instead." She nodded reluctantly as Nigel took off in pursuit of Krampus. I was on his heels.

"Park the car," I told Diane.

I ran hard behind Nigel and Krampus as they made their way through the streets of Key West until they eventually reached a small alleyway near the harbor. I watched Nigel catch Krampus, grab him by the shoulder, and spin him around. They both fell to the pavement in the process. Nigel was quick to his feet as Krampus rose to confront him.

"You two think you can catch me, don't you? Well, you can't because you're not true disciples of Christmas.

"Nigel, you think you believe, but you're only kidding yourself. And you know it. If you were, you would have found Sinter and Sylvia before now."

"Well," said Nigel, "I'll tell you something that I do believe."

Nigel took two steps, and with some of the quickest hands I've ever witnessed, delivered two powerful righthand blows to Krampus's jaw. Then he followed with a left that sent Krampus down to the ground. Nigel stood over him.

"I believe I'll knock your head off if you don't tell us what you've done with them. Now, where are they, dammit! I've had about enough of your ugly ass."

Krampus stood and laughed in Nigel's face. Then he turned to me. "And, Cam, you *know* you don't follow the spirit of Christmas. You've said it many times. I represent a very large part of Christmas. If you believed in me, you would understand. Christmas is dead to the two of you," he snickered.

Nigel took another swing, but Krampus disappeared in a plume of smoke as his fist drove through it. Nigel stomped. "Dammit!"

Then we heard yelling down the street. People were fighting again.

"He's moved down the street," I said.

Just as we were about to run toward the yelling crowd, Dietmar caught up with us. "Where'd he go?" he asked, puffing slightly from his run.

I pointed to the crowd. "That way."

"Did you talk to him?"

"Yes, he said we weren't true disciples, so we could never catch him."

"But Nigel, you've met Sinter, and you know he is the real article."

"I do. And Krampus has one hard head."

"You hit him? You actually touched him?"

"Yeah, three times. He went down."

"And?"

Nigel looked at me, and I said, "Nothing. Didn't faze him. He laughed."

"Still," said Dietmar, "the fact Nigel made physical contact tells me his faith is stronger than he knows."

"And you, Cam. Do you believe yet?"

"I believe there's something out there. But Sinter? Not yet."

"How could there be a Krampus if there's no Sinter? That would be like believing in the Devil but not God."

"That, I don't know. All I know is there is an evil spirit on the streets, and we must contain it."

Dietmar said, "According to legend, he is the son of Hel, the Norse god of the underworld. He is a strong spirit but until now has only used it against naughty children. He's up to something."

The crowd down the street had stopped fighting now and returned to partying.

Nigel said, "He told me if I were a believer, I would have already found them."

"What does that tell you?" Dietmar asked.

"I don't know."

"Did Sinter give you any clues as to where Krampus might take them?"

"He mentioned Christmas Key. It's supposed to be near here. I guess one of his many churches is located there."

"Christmas Key?" Dietmar said. "That's where we must take Krampus. We have to get him before the Christmas parade."

"That's what Sinter said," Nigel agreed.

Diane showed up a minute later. "I had a hard time finding a parking place. Did you get him?"

"No," I said. "He got away again."

"How do we ever expect to capture him if he can disappear at will?" Nigel asked Dietmar.

"If you're a true believer, you'll weaken him. Then we can tie his hands. Without the use of his hands, he is helpless. But, as long as the two of you don't believe."

"But I do believe," Nigel said. "I've talked to Sinter."

"True, you believe in Sinter, but do you really believe in God? That is the true meaning of Christmas."

"Yes, I do," Nigel said, but he didn't sound convincing.

"So do Diane and I," I said.

"Maybe that's your answer then."

"You're talking in riddles," I said. "What's our answer?"

"God."

I shook my head. He wasn't making any sense. I was starting to wonder if he was a hunter at all. He hasn't confronted Krampus once. The places he took us to find him were full of the Christmas spirit. If we're going to find Krampus, we need to find people fighting.

We all stood in silence, trying to figure out the clues we had. I spoke up first.

"We need to find this... Christmas Key."

"But we've never heard of it," Nigel said. "How are we going to find it?"

"We can take my plane and fly over the area. I've flown over the Keys many times, but I wasn't looking for anything out of the ordinary. Maybe there's a clue."

"But we would have to wait until morning," Dietmar said. "That might be too late."

"If it's really a Christmas Key," I said, "don't you think it would be lit up? It would be easy to spot at night."

"I'll go with Cam," Dietmar said. "You two check the streets again and if you see anything, call us."

We all agreed splitting up would be better than everyone hanging together. If we spread out, our chances would be increased greatly.

Twenty-One

Once in the air, I circled Key West in a tight pattern. I flew the coast as far as Marathon then cut over to the gulf side and came back toward Key West.

"I'm going out a mile and make another loop," I said.

Dietmar looked at his watch. "Go out two miles," he said. "We'll still be able to see the lights."

I widened my search. I thought about what I was doing. Searching for Santa Claus.

"It's not that strange when you think about it," he said.

"What's not?"

"Searching for Sinter. You did that a lot as a child, didn't you?"

"How did you know I was thinking about that?"

"I could tell by the look on your face. You're starting to believe, or you wouldn't be out here."

"I'm starting to wonder what it is that makes all of us think we've seen Krampus and Sinter."

"Believing."

I sighed heavily. "I guess."

"There," Dietmar said. "Look at that island."

I looked down and saw it. It was all lit up with red and green lights.

"I don't ever remember seeing that island before," I said.

"Then that must be it. That's Christmas Key," Dietmar said.

I banked right, flew away from the island, then banked back toward it as I lost altitude. We flew over the island at two hundred feet, barely missing the tall pine trees that were covered with lights.

The island was small, with a village nestled among the trees. The buildings were all made of wood and brightly painted in reds, greens, blues, and whites. There was a church at the center of the village with a tall steeple that rose up to meet the stars.

We flew over the village once more before turning back toward Key West to get my boat to take us back to the island.

We had found Christmas Key, but our journey was not over yet. We still had to find Krampus or Sinter if they were indeed there. But we knew that we would have to return soon to find out what mysteries this island held for us.

"Did you notice anything unusual about the island?" Dietmar asked.

"Everything about the island was unusual."

"You know what I mean."

"The snow?"

Diane and Nigel walked the streets of old town Key West. SantaCon was still in full swing as they made their way toward Sloppy Joe's. If the people were partying earlier, then they were completely wasted now. The streets were packed with drunken revelers in Santa hats and elf costumes.

As they walked, Diane noticed a group of six elves standing stiffly in their infectious costumes outside a building. They were whispering amongst themselves and watching the crowd suspiciously.

"Nigel," she whispered, "do you see those guys over there?"

"Yeah, what about them?"

"Don't they look a bit out of place among the party-goers?"

Nigel looked over and studied the group. He had to admit that something was off; their presence felt intrusive.

"I don't know, but we should keep an eye on them."

They continued on their way, but Diane couldn't shake the feeling that they were being followed

As they approached Sloppy Joe's, another rowdy band of elves stumbled out of the bar, almost knocking them over. One of the elves turned to them with glassy eyes and slurred, "You guys wanna come in and have a drink with us?"

Nigel politely declined, and they continued on their way. As they walked away, Diane noticed the group of elves still behind them, almost as if they were trailing them.

"Nigel, we're being followed. We need to lose them.

They picked up their pace and started running down the street. The elves followed close behind.

They pulled into an alley and hid behind a dumpster just as the elves rounded the corner. Fortunately for them, the costume-clad men didn't notice that they had stopped running.

"What the hell was that about?" Nigel said breathlessly.

"I don't know, but it looks as if Krampus has some help. Let's get out of here before things get any worse."

They returned to Duval Street and made their way to Front Street, where they walked toward the docks. They walked the dock until they arrived at the Conch Republic Seafood bar. Just as they stepped inside, they heard a commotion behind them and spun around to see another fight breaking out between two men while a large group watched and cheered in intoxication. Ignoring it completely, they took two of the three empty stools at the bar.

The bartender came to where they were sitting. She was a young red-haired girl that had been working there since Nigel had come to town nine months ago.

"Hey Nigel, what'll it be? The usual?" she hollered over the crowd.

He looked at Diane.

"I'll have a Corona," she said.

Bridget threw up two thumbs instead of yelling over the crowd. Thirty seconds later, Bridget sat a Corona in front of Diane and a Diet Coke for Nigel. He held up his hand and motioned for Bridget to lean over the bar as he did the same. "Do you remember the man who was sitting next to me last night? Old guy with a white beard, funny clothes, and hat."

"You mean Kris. Yeah, I remember."

"Has he been back in here?"

She shook her head. "Did he tell you he was Santa?"

Nigel nodded.

She laughed, "He's crazy. He comes here a lot, but I haven't seen him today."

"Thanks," he said and turned back to Diane. He shrugged.

"I think I know who you're talking about now," Diane said, looking around the area. "One time he told Stacy and me that his name was Pere Noel. We googled him when we got home, and that's another name for Santa Claus in Canada. We got a big laugh out of it at the time. He's been coming around here this time every year forever. Maybe he'll be back in here soon."

"I don't think so. Not if Krampus has him. We've got to figure out where he would have locked them up."

"Didn't Krampus say, if you were a believer, you would have already found them?"

Nigel nodded again. Then they both stared at each other. Their eyes got bigger as it came to them.

They jumped off the stools and ran out of the bar. Once outside, where they could talk without yelling, Nigel asked, "Where's the closest church?"

"He won't be there. He goes to the Key West United Methodist Church. I've seen him there. It's the only church large enough to hide someone. It's about six blocks from here. Let's go."

They ran the six blocks and burst into the church. Pastor McDaniel was standing inside the church arranging the songbooks in the pews.

"Here, here," he said when the two intruded. "What's going on?"

"We think Sylvia Mason is here," Nigel said.

"She was here last Sunday," the pastor said, "but I haven't seen her since."

"Are you sure?"

"What's this all about?"

"We think she was kidnapped along with Kris Kringle."

Obviously amused, McDaniel said, "Really? By whom, the Grinch?" he laughed.

"No... I mean, yeah," Diane said. "We think it was Krampus."

The pastor took in the faces of the two. "Diane, I think you're serious."

"I am. I know it sounds crazy, but we do believe."

"What do you believe in?"

"Sinter, Krampus, God; we believe in all of it."

He smiled, amused. "Kris has done it again. He makes different people believe every year. Just the fact that you're here, in my church, shows me what is in your hearts."

"Do you know Sinter?" Nigel asked.

"Oh, yes. Kris took me in years ago. I was chasing Krampus around town, trying to perform an exorcism on him. I never caught him. He would disappear every time I got close."

"Yeah, that's what happens with us," Diane said.

"Let me guess," he said, "Cam is tied up in all of this too, right?"

"Yes, he's out with a man named Dietmar right now trying to find Christmas Key."

The pastor smiled. "I know where Christmas Key is and I'm sure Cam will know when he returns. It's a wondrous place, filled with snow-covered trees and magical creatures. The sky is lit up with stars that sparkle like diamonds in the night. You can hear the laughter of children playing in the snow, and you can smell the sweet scent of pine needles as they fill the air, and a huge temple that stands tall over it all. It truly is a magical place. But you must be careful when you go there; Krampus has been known to wander these lands looking for troublemakers."

"Krampus goes to Christmas Key?" Diane asked.

"No, he won't go near that place, but he'll block your way if he can."

Nigel asked, "Is there any way we can get Krampus to Christmas Key?"

"It can happen. Even Krampus has his weaknesses, but I'm too old to chase after those spirits again."

"How can we get him there?"

"First, you must find five or more people who honestly believe in Sinter and then contact Krampus. You also must have children with you. That is his main weakness, naughty children. If he can't find naughty children, he'll punish the good ones for ruining his fun. He will follow you there. Once you're there, the power of Christianity will keep Krampus at bay. Christmas Key is a place of peace and joy, and it's been that way for centuries. I wish you luck on your journey."

The pastor smiled as he watched the two leave his church, inspired by his words. He knew that if they tried to follow his direction, they would fail. But in doing so, they would realize what they really must do, and Krampus would follow them all the way to Christmas Key. He looked up to the sky and said a silent prayer for their success before closing up shop for the night.

I put the phone on speaker and called Diane as soon as we landed. "I think we found Christmas Key," I said.

"Good. We just came from the church. The pastor told us how to get Krampus."

"Did he tell you to gather five or more believers?" Dietmar interrupted.

"Yes," she said.

"That won't work. He tried that a long time ago and still swears that one of them was not a believer."

I looked at Dietmar. "You've tried to catch him here before?"

"It was fifteen years ago. Now I am stronger and know more."

"Are you sure, Dietmar," Diane said. "The pastor seemed to be sincere."

"He was sincere, but wrong."

"Then how will we get Krampus to Christmas Key?" I asked.

Dietmar sighed, "The only person who can get him there is Sinter."

"How do we get Sinter free so he can catch Krampus?"

"I believe that Krampus has hidden Sinter and Sylvia on Christmas Key. I think he has hidden him in the least obvious place. If we make it known that we are going there to free them, he might come there to stop us. But, if he gets there before we can free them, we'll have to deal with him ourselves."

"We have to take the chance," I said. "We can't let Sinter and Sylvia stay locked up until after Christmas. There won't be any Christmas. That would ruin the world. It's a holy night for all countries that unites the people."

Dietmar smiled at me. "We can do it now, I'm sure."

Twenty-Two

We arranged to meet Diane and Nigel on Duval Street. Somehow, we needed to put the word out that we were going to Christmas Key to save Santa. That was going to be easier said than done. Everyone would think we were crazy. Me included.

We met them outside Sloppy Joe's since it was more central to where the action was. It was after ten now. I thought maybe the crowd would thin out, but it was heavier than a few hours ago.

"How are we going to get Krampus to pay any attention to us?" Diane asked. "We're never going to get him to hear that we're going to Christmas Key."

There was a band stage set up in the street now. A few musicians were tuning their instruments and checking the mics.

"I have an idea," I said.

I went to the stage and climbed the steps. I was stopped by a man who had been moving an amplifier around the stage.

"Woo there, big fella," he said. "You need to get off the stage."

"I have an announcement to make, then I'll leave peacefully," I said, standing as tall and menacing as I could. Then I felt the steps move and turned to see Nigel had climbed them too.

The man looked between the two of us. I saw his shoulders drop. He was tired and ready to go home. "Make it quick," he growled and fidgeted with a button on his coat.

I walked to the mic, still trying to figure out what I was going to say. When I opened my mouth, the words came out as if a thought had crystallized in my head and burst forth unedited. "Excuse me. Your attention, please!" My voice boomed through the speakers and made him jump.

A few patrons stopped in their tracks and turned their heads toward me, then began gossiping amongst themselves.

"Your attention, please!" I called again, this time with more gusto than before, projecting my voice over theirs so that they could hear me above the din of happy chatter and rowdy laughter. A hush fell over them for a moment.

Now every pair of eyes was on mine. There was no longer any banter fluting back from one table to another across the street or low talk about where people would go next after leaving here tonight. They seemed interested in what I had to say, which encouraged me to continue.

"Thank you. I wanted to let you know that we are going to go now and bring you the real Santa."

"Sinter," Nigel said, who was standing beside me.

We got a lot of laughs and also quite a few cheers.

"Don't go away," I continued, "We know where he is, and we're going to Christmas Key to get him. He'll be here within the hour. Believe me; you don't want to miss this."

More cheers came from the crowd, which had grown to most of the block now.

"Let's go, Cam," Nigel said. "Before they start throwing things at us."

We got off the stage as fast as we could.

Dietmar was waiting. "That sounded like a trap. Do you think Krampus will fall for it?"

"I think if we're right, he'll have no choice but to go there. Let's get to the boat as fast as we can."

"Where's Diane?" I asked.

We looked around the crowd.

"She must have wandered off," Nigel said. "I'll find her. You guys get the boat ready."

We arrived at the dock, but Diane and Nigel had yet to show up. As we approached my boat, Stacy emerged from her cabin with Walter and Hank trailing behind. She waved at us cheerfully before calling out a greeting. Walter bounded towards me and eagerly lapped up some attention. He then began growling aggressively at Dietmar and bared his teeth in a menacing display. A deep rumble escaped Hank's throat as he mirrored Walter's behavior. Red-faced, I commanded them to stop and apologized for their rudeness. Dietmar seemed unfazed by the unsavory welcome, politely greeting Stacy with a nod of his head and a "Mademoiselle"—which made her smile. Not wanting any more drama, Stacy grabbed hold of Hank's collar and ushered him back inside.

I saw a flash of light and looked toward the lot. Diane and Nigel were getting out of a cab.

"What's up?" Stacy asked now that she saw everyone was there. "Are you having a party on your boat?"

"No," I said, "we have some business to take care of. We should be back in a few hours."

"Do you want me to keep Walter for the rest of the night?"

I glanced at Walter and then Dietmar, who was watching Walter closely. "No, I think I'll take him with me. I'm sure you have plans to go out anyway."

"No, I was out earlier. It's a jungle. Ryan was just here. He went to get us a pizza. We're staying in."

"Ryan? How'd he get here so fast?"

"What do you mean? He's been here all evening."

"Oh." *How can that be? We just saw him in Sugarloaf.* "I just thought he'd be working tonight with all that was going on."

"No, he got off work at three o'clock. Early shift."

Diane and Nigel stepped onto the dock and were greeted by Walter. Then he turned his stare back to Dietmar.

"Are we ready?" I asked.

"The question is," Dietmar said, "Are *you* ready?"

"What do ya mean?"

"You told that crowd that you were going to bring the real Santa," then looking at Nigel, "Sinter. Does this mean you're starting to come around, Cam?"

I hadn't given it a thought when I was on stage. There for a minute, I was sure of myself. "So, yeah. Maybe, a little."

Diane spoke up, "I'm starting to believe."

"You all know where I stand," said Nigel.

"How do you know that the island you saw was Christmas Key?" Diane asked.

As we walked to my boat, I described it to them. "Then, to cap it off," I said, "It was snowing."

"Snowing?" she said.

"That's right," Dietmar said. "We saw it."

"And you think that Sinter and Sylvia are there?"

I nodded my head slightly at Diane. She looked away and mouthed, "Wow."

"Over the years of hunting for Krampus," Dietmar said, "I've learned that only true believers can see anything related to Sinter. I know him personally. I have met him many times—actually, every year. No one else can see Christmas Key. You've flown over this area for years and have probably cruised your boat right through where the Key sits. Have you ever seen it before?"

"No, you're right about that. This is the first time."

"That's because you believe now."

"We'll see," I said, but I didn't even sound convincing to myself.

Onboard, Diane and Nigel flipped the lines loose and coiled them on the deck while I started the engines. Using my thrusters, I eased away from the dock, then, under power, we headed through the mouth of the small marina.

The moon was high in the sky now, and the stars were exceptionally bright. One star gleamed in the sky as if it were alive. It truly looked as if it were a Christmas night right out of a storybook.

"Can you find the Key?" Nigel asked from behind me.

"Yeah, I know exactly where it is. It'll take us about a half-hour. We have to pass Dredgers Key and into Jawfish Basin. Once we're out there, we can open it up a bit, but it's still dangerous waters. I'll have to keep an eye on the gauges since it's too dark to see the water's color."

"Let me know if you need any help."

We finished speaking, but Nigel stood there beside me. He was looking at the star I had noticed. I glanced at him and saw the look.

"I know," I said, "That's right where we're headed."

"Believing is an eerie thing, isn't it?"

"It's getting that way. I can't get over the fact that we're heading out in the middle of the night to rescue Sinter from Krampus. Those words just don't sound real."

Nigel changed the subject. "Do you think we'll be friends when this is over?"

"We already are."

"So, you don't think I'm crazy anymore?"

"I think we both are."

"Can I ask Diane out sometime?"

"Don't press your luck, pal."

We were silent for a while, then I said, "Stacy told me a while ago that Ryan had been at her place all evening. We just saw him at Sugarloaf."

"Yeah, he was there with your friend Dave."

"I'm going to call Dave. Just to check."

I called Dave on his cell phone. He answered on the second ring.

"Cam, where are you? This place is hoppin' tonight."

"Where are you?"

"I'm workin' at Schooners like every other night."

"Have you been there all night?"

"Since noon."

"Okay, just checking. I might be there later."

I hung up and looked at Nigel. "He's been at work since noon."

We were silent as we both turned and looked at the bright star that was guiding our way.

Twenty-Three

The boat cut through the water as we made our way to Christmas Key. The air was cool and smelled of salt, and the sound of the waves lapping against the hull was soothing. We discussed our plans for when we reached Sinter, trying to come up with a way to save him from Krampus. We talked about ways to distract Krampus or even better, capture him and take him back with us. Our ideas grew more outlandish as time went on, but nothing seemed foolproof enough yet.

The sky was beginning to lighten now, and I could make out the outline of the mysterious island in the distance. As we got closer, I could see that it wasn't what I had expected; it looked like a small tropical paradise with white sandy beaches and crystal-clear waters. Despite its beauty, there was an eerie feeling in the air, as if something sinister lurked just beneath the surface.

As we pulled to the dock, I saw that I was mistaken. The white sand was actually snow, gleaming in the early sun.

We tied up at the nearby dock and disembarked silently. We each took a deep breath before heading off into the unknown—whatever awaited us on Christmas Key would be our fate now.

Diane bent down and made a snowball. "I haven't seen snow in years," she said excitedly.

I couldn't resist the temptation to get a handful myself. I made a perfect snowball, then reared back and let it fly. I hit Nigel square in the back. Everyone laughed.

Nigel, not to be outdone, made his own snowball and sailed it back at me. Before I could get out of the way, it hit me on the side of my head. Diane threw hers at Nigel, catching him on the arm. Dietmar took up Nigel's side, and we had a good old fashion snowball fight.

It ended with all of us breathing hard and laughing. Then when we were silent again, we turned to take in the scenery. I saw Walter running and jumping, landing head-first in a snowbank.

The giant pine trees were covered with snow, and the colorful twinkling lights made the island look truly... well, Christmassy.

I thought about what was happening for a minute, then turning to the others, said, "Sinter is real, isn't he? I truly believe he's real."

"You're right, Cam. He has always been here," Dietmar said. "This is the Christmas setting you remember, right?"

I nodded. "Yes, I remember it like it was yesterday."

We began our search for Sinter. We searched the small huts that surrounded the church that towered over the island. We searched the beaches and snow-covered trails, calling out his name as we went.

As we walked, I noticed something strange—there were no people on Christmas Key. Not a single soul in sight. It was as if everyone had vanished without a trace. All the huts were lit, and smoke came from the chimneys, but no people.

We stopped and huddled together in the center of the square where the church sat. I turned to look at it.

"Listen," I said. "I can hear music."

There was soft Christmas music coming from inside the church.

"Let's check it out."

I led the way to the front door of the giant church. The wooden doors were at least fifteen feet tall, but when I touched one of them, it swung open with ease.

The music grew louder as the door swung. The church was packed with parishioners. Children and adults.

I heard a low growl come from Dietmar. Diane placed her hand on his shoulder, and he stopped. He looked down at her, and she shook her head. He nodded.

The singers turned to look at us. They had rosy cheeks and big smiles. A few of them motioned for us to come inside and join them.

We did. I started to sing as we made our way toward a pew with four empty spaces. We sang two Christmas songs before there was a break. I didn't think that this could be anything other than the North Pole that I remembered as a kid.

Then a figure rose from the sanctuary and walked to the podium. It was Sinter. I looked at Nigel and Diane. "He's here," I said.

It was the Kris I knew from the bars every year. Diane laughed slightly. "He was telling the truth all this time, and we doubted him."

"Isn't it beautiful?" a voice from beside me sounded.

Nigel and I looked at the same time. Sylvia was standing between us. She placed her hand on Nigel's arm and kissed him.

I noticed that Walter wasn't around. Then I saw him heading to the sanctuary. In front of him was Dietmar. He was reluctantly making his way to the front of the church. Walter was nipping at his heels, making sure he kept moving.

"Come on up, Dietmar," Sinter said. "You have done a good thing."

As he climbed the steps to the sanctuary, Sinter looked our way and waved.

"Diane, Cam, and Nigel, we are glad to see that you have come to join us. We've been waiting for you to find your way. And don't forget, you told the people you would bring them the real Sinter. I might not be able to make it to the stage, but I will be there."

Dietmar moved to the side of Sinter with Walter's help.

"Thank you, Walter," Sinter said.

Walter turned and ran back to me. The laughter of the people following him.

"Well, folks," Sinter said, "I guess we'll have to put up with Krampus for another year. He has delivered as promised."

Sinter stepped away from Dietmar and nodded. Dietmar raised his hands as smoke surrounded him. When the smoke cleared, Krampus was standing there. Everyone cheered, and Sinter hugged him.

I looked at Diane, "You knew he was Krampus."

"I wasn't sure until we arrived here. But I always wondered why we never saw them at the same time."

"Everything he did was to make believers out of the three of us. Making Dave and Ryan appear on the beach. Tony Wilks and Glen Clem were even friends. That should have told me right there that something wasn't right."

I couldn't believe what I was hearing. Sinter and Krampus were real, and they had been orchestrating everything that had happened to us over the past few days. I looked around the church, still in shock that I was standing here witnessing this.

Sinter stepped forward again. "It's time for the final part of our celebration. Are you ready, my friends?"

We nodded, unsure of what was to come. As we were leaving the chapel, Nigel asked Sinter, "Why the small band of elves? They were chasing us."

"Those were Drows, or dark elves. They could sense that you were on your way to believing. You're lucky they didn't catch you. You wouldn't have been here to see this."

"What if they come for us again?"

"They can't touch you now. You are believers, and much power comes with that."

Sinter led us out of the church and onto the beach. The snow had disappeared, replaced once again with white sand and crystal-clear water. In the distance, I could see a large bonfire burning brightly.

As we approached, I could see that there were more people there, all gathered around the fire, singing, and dancing.

Sinter turned to us. "This is our final celebration of the year. We welcome the new year with open hearts and open minds. We celebrate life, love, and the spirit of Christmas." Then he waved his hand, and the air filled with sparkling confetti that rained down on us.

I felt a warmth spreading through me, and I realized that this was where I belonged. This was my home.

We joined in the singing and dancing, forgetting about everything else. As the early morning wore on, I felt a peace settling over me. I knew that I would never forget this moment and that I would always carry it with me.

As the sun began to rise, Sinter appeared before us once more. "It's time for us to part ways, my friends. But know that you are always welcome here, on Christmas Key."

We said our goodbyes, and, with Sylvia, we boarded our boat. I looked back at the island, but the island was gone. Just as it had appeared out of nowhere, it vanished again without a trace. It was bittersweet to leave this magical place, but I knew that I would always carry the memories with me.

As we sailed away, I couldn't help but feel grateful for the experience. I had found something here that I had been searching for my whole life—a sense of belonging, a sense of magic.

I sipped on Wild Turkey while Nigel got loopy on Diet Coke. We talked while Diane and Sylvia captained the boat. We knew now that we had a special bond, and we would always be friends.

"Let's get together for supper next week," Nigel said.

"That sounds good," I said. "I'm buying."

As the boat rocked gently on the waves, I leaned back against the railing and looked up at the sky. The stars twinkled brightly, and I felt a sense of wonder fill me.

I knew that this was only the beginning of my adventure. There were so many more stories to be told, so many more mysteries to uncover.

And as I closed my eyes and let the sea breeze wash over me, I knew that I was ready for whatever lay ahead.

"Cam!" I was startled out of my sleep. "Cam," Stacy said. "Sorry to wake you, but could you watch Hank for me today? I've been called in to work."

Trying to wipe the numbness from my brain, I said, "Sure, no problem."

Then I sat up and looked around. I was alone on my boat. "Did you see Diane leaving?" I asked her.

"No. I haven't seen her around here all day. Are you okay?"

I thought about what I had just been through. Was all of that a dream? No, I don't think so.

"Cam?"

"Yeah, yeah, come here, Hank."

Hank came to me, and I petted him. "He can spend the night."

Stacy bent down and kissed me. Then she wiped something from my shirt. "What do you have all over you?" she asked, picking a piece of something red off of me. "Where'd you get all these confetti?"

I chuckled as I thought about Sinter throwing it in the air.

"What's so funny?" she asked.

Then I started to laugh uncontrollably.

"You're weird, Cam. I'll see you in the morning."

It was a relief to know that what had happened yesterday was real. But now, I had to deal with the fact that Sinter is a real person. This will change my life.

I called Diane to make sure she was okay. I remember dropping her off at her house last night, but I don't remember much after that.

"Diane, are you all right? I was worried about you."

"Yes, I'm fine."

"Would you like to get together with Sylvia and Nigel for supper tonight? We all have a lot to catch up on."

"That sounds good to me. I need to get some of the details straight. My mind must be slipping."

"I'll call Nigel and set it up."

Nigel answered on the first ring. "Hey Cam, I was just getting ready to call you," he said.

"Great minds think alike. I was just calling to see if you and Sylvia would like to get together with Diane and me."

"That's what I had in mind. How about the Conch Republic Seafood Company?" Nigel suggested.

"Works for me. See ya around six?"

"Sounds good. We need to talk."

Diane and I arrived at five-forty-five and saw Nigel and Sylvia already sipping drinks.

They stood when we approached the table and hugged us.

After ordering and testing our drinks, we broke into a conversation.

We talked about Krampus and Sinter all night long. Everyone shared their stories of what happened during our time on the Key, but slowly our memories were fading away like a dream. We laughed at some of the things that happened but also felt sad that it was all coming to an end so soon.

"How did we end up in Germany?" I asked.

"You found the portal in the basement of that room," Nigel explained.

"Yeah, but what room? Where the hell were we? Why did Krampus lead us there?"

Diane interrupted, "I think the more that happened to you, the more you recognized the truth. They were pulling you in. When they were sure you believed, they led you to Christmas Key."

Sylvia said, "The time I spent on Christmas Key with Sinter, he kept telling me that the three of you would be coming that evening. Once in a while, he would lean over to me and say, "They're almost here. I think they believe." He would stop occasionally and listen, then talk back to someone who wasn't there."

"That must have been when Dietmar would get out of the car and talk. They were scheming," I said.

We finished off our meal with a round of hot chocolate before heading down the dock to Schooner Wharf Bar for a nightcap. As we walked back together in silence, I couldn't help but feel grateful for the amazing experience we'd just been through together—one that would stay with me forever, no matter how hard I tried to forget it.

Twenty-Four

When we spoke, the air stood solid around us. The conversation was a haze of words whose meanings were lost in transit as if we didn't simply have a meal together—as if we'd been through something. Something had changed us, and now there was nothing to talk about. I couldn't remember why we were here or what it was that we had done together.

As though we all came to the same realization at the same time, Diane said, "Oh look, there's that Kris guy that always claims to be Santa Claus."

He sat at a table for five and waved us over with one hand while he held his drink in the other. We stopped in front of him and greeted each other with hugs. His smile stretched so wide that I noticed the creases in his face and the crow's feet near his eyes became more noticeable.

He patted each of our shoulders and whispered, "What you are doing is good. Have a seat."

I noticed a strange twinkle in his blue eyes as he looked from one person to another. He drew us in with his smile like water from an underground spring bubbling up to the surface of the water-starved earth. "*Santa*?" I thought to myself, but I figured it was just a joke. A prank.

"Have you children been busy getting ready for Christmas?" he asked my friends and me.

Diane jumped into the conversation before anyone else had a chance to say anything. "No," she blurted out, then paused for a moment and continued, "Well, not really. I mean, yes—sort of—I'm almost finished, though." She turned her head away from him slightly and gave me an embarrassed glance as she deciphered her thoughts aloud for everyone to hear. "I still want to get something for the children who won't receive presents this year."

"Do you believe?" he asked Diane with straight-faced seriousness, which startled me deeply because somehow, I felt like he knew how important this question was to us all right now... How much meaning this answer held for all of us for some reason, I kept thinking, what are we supposed to say? Diane wasn't expecting this question either; there were tears welling up in her eyes when she answered him.

"Yes, I do."

"So do I," I added quickly without hesitation while nodding my head vigorously in agreement with Diane's belief because I had always followed along with whatever Diane believed completely, whether or not it made sense—even if it meant deep trouble later on because I didn't know any better than she did at that point, we both figure everything would work out later—somehow someway—no matter how bad things got, we still stuck together side by side (throughout thick and thin).

"Yes," Nigel said, "He likes to be called Sinter."

"That's right," Sylvia said.

Kris leaned back in his chair and let out a jolly, "Ho, Ho, Ho!"

We looked at him, as did the rest of the people in the open-air restaurant.

Nigel scrunched up his face. "Ho, Ho, Ho? Where did that come from?"

Sinter shrugged his shoulders and said, "Well... if you can't beat 'em." Then he laughed from somewhere deep in his belly.

When he finished, his face was red, and his grin had grown even wider. His eyes sparkled with an intensity of mischief that I couldn't quite put my finger on. It was as if he knew something that we didn't, something that would change everything we thought we knew about Christmas.

"I have a proposition for you all," he said, his voice low and conspiratorial. "Something that will make this Christmas one to remember."

We leaned in closer, intrigued by his words. What could he possibly have in mind?

"I want you to help me spread the magic of Christmas," he continued. "To bring joy and happiness to those who need it most."

We nodded eagerly, caught up in his enthusiasm. Whatever he had planned, we were willing to help. But why? Days before, we thought this man was just fantasizing about being Santa, and now, it seemed we thought he might really be Sinter.

"Excellent," he said, clapping his hands together. "Let's get started."

And with that, we followed him out of the restaurant and into the bustling streets of Key West, ready to spread the magic of Christmas wherever it was needed. As we walked, I couldn't help but feel a sense of excitement and wonder bubbling up inside of me. This Christmas was going to be different but in the best possible way.

As we walked, Sinter led us to a small alleyway that was hidden away from the main street. He pulled out a large sack from behind his back and placed it on the ground before us.

"Take a look inside," he said, grinning mischievously.

Curiosity getting the better of us, we eagerly opened the sack and peered inside. It was filled to the brim with colorful presents wrapped in shiny paper and tied with glittering ribbons.

"Whose are these?" Sylvia asked, her eyes wide with wonder.

"They're for the children who won't be receiving any gifts this year," Sinter replied, his voice full of compassion. "The ones who have been forgotten or overlooked. But we're going to change that."

We all nodded in agreement, touched by his kindness. Without hesitation, we started to distribute the presents to anyone we saw who looked like they needed a little bit of Christmas magic in their lives.

As we moved through the town, giving out presents to strangers, I couldn't help but feel a sense of joy and fulfillment. This was what Christmas was truly about, spreading love and kindness to those who needed it most. And with Sinter leading the way, we were making a real difference in people's lives.

As the night wore on, we found ourselves handing out the last of the presents. With heavy hearts, we started to make our way back to the restaurant, feeling a sense of loss now that our mission was complete.

But as we turned the corner, we were met with a sight that took our breath away. The entire street was lit up with twinkling lights and festive decorations, and in the center of it all stood a magnificent Christmas tree. It was the most beautiful thing I had ever seen.

Sinter grinned at us knowingly. "I have one more surprise for you," he said, leading us toward the tree.

As we got closer, we noticed that there were small presents nestled in the branches, each one with a tag bearing our names. We eagerly plucked them from the tree and unwrapped them, laughing and squealing with delight like children on Christmas morning.

It was then that I realized that this was the best Christmas I had ever had. Not because of the presents we had received, but because of the love and kindness we had given to others. And as we stood there, surrounded by the twinkling lights and the sounds of carolers singing in the distance, I knew that this was a memory I would cherish for the rest of my life.

"It is more blessed to give than to receive" Jesus, according to Paul.

Never The End
From Kirk and Mac...
Merry Christmas!

About the Author

KIRK JOCKELL

Kirk Jockell is an American writer and the creator of The Nigel Logan Action Series. He lives in Port St. Joe, Florida, where he patiently waits for his wife to retire, so she can join him for a simpler life down on The Forgotten Coast. Kirk is a sailor and an avid photographer of sailboats. He loves to fish, throw his cast net for mullet, listen to music (Pop Country doesn't count), play his guitar, and drive his Bronco on the beach. Kirk lives with his lovely wife Joy, a rescued bluetick coonhound named Nate (#98Nate), and a tuxedo cat named Mr. Hemingway.

Visit Kirk at www.KirkJockell.com

About the Author

Mac Fortner

Mac Fortner is a Tropical Adventure Author who was born in Evansville, Indiana but was never one to hang around one area too long. He lived for eighteen months in the Philippine islands and a year in Saigon. When he returned to Evansville, he spent time on his boats on the Ohio River.

This only fed his thirst for adventure, and he now lives in Florida three months out of the year with his wife, Cindy.

They love spending time traveling the Florida Keys, where his protagonist, Cam Derringer, finds trouble around every turn.

He has been a full-time author since 2015 and now writes overlooking the beach and the Gulf of Mexico but longs for the time when he can call Key West home.

You can join Mac's newsletter at www.macofortner.com and get your free prequel to the series. There you will be informed when a new book or new deal is coming out.

Visit Mac at www.MacoFortner.com

Made in the USA
Monee, IL
28 December 2024